AS YOU STEP OUTSIDE

By the same author:

The Comedienne

The Woman in Beige

Diary of a Provincial Lesbian

AS YOU STEP OUTSIDE

VG LEE

Tollington

To my primary friend, Mary V

First published by Tollington Press, London, 2008
www.tollingtonpress.co.uk

A catalogue record for this book is available from the British Library.

ISBN 978-0-9560173-0-7

Cover photograph by Les Kinch
Cover design by Sarah Wood
Typeset in Stone by Helen Sandler
Printed and bound in the UK by Biddles

'A Slice of Melon' was first published in *Va-Va-Voom: Red Hot Lesbian Erotica* (Red Hot Diva, 2004); an abridged version of 'Shush' was first published in *Chroma* journal Issue 4 (2006); 'The Passing Guest' was first published in *Necrologue: The Diva Book of the Dead and the Undead* (Diva, 2003); 'Shirley Poppy' was first published in *Fish Anthology 2004: Spoonface & Other Stories*; 'The Holiday Let' first appeared in *Groundswell: The Diva Book of Short Stories 2* (Diva, 2002) and later, in a different form, as part of a novel, *The Woman in Beige* (Diva, 2003); 'Unknown Woman with Bird and Pomegranate' was first published in *Mslexia* (October 2007); 'Swallowtail' was first published in *Il Duce's Match, Rome 1940: Winner's Anthology, Writers Inc. Writer of the Year Competition* (2003).

Contents

Holding out for a Hero

I noticed her hair first because it was glossy and the other women's hair was dull and stiff with lacquer. It snaked in dark blonde coils to her shoulders. She should have had bigger hair, like, say, *Charlie's Angels*. Big hair of that quality would have looked stupendous; instead at the front it hung limply around her face and as the evening wore on it got flatter and more untidy.

She was in her late twenties, squashed into hipster, black leather trousers and a skin-tight, see-through shirt. She wore her clothes with the confidence of a woman who'd once known her figure was desirably voluptuous. That must have been at least five kilos ago. Her name was Karen.

"Karen, what you having?" someone asked.

"Vodka tonic."

Later the bar ran out of tonic.

Better say now, while all this observation was going on, I was standing in the ballroom at the end of Hastings pier. It's a fleapit of a pier although the council refers to it as 'Covent Garden on Sea', since it was refurbished a few years back. I hadn't been able to bag one of the chairs arranged around the circular tables at the edge of the dance floor, so I had to stand, my shoulders against a barred and padlocked fire door.

Each time I moved, my feet came off the carpet with a nasty sucking sensation. Outside it was December and freezing cold, inside stifling. The ballroom was packed, at least a thousand people, ages ranging from twenty to sixty, women dressed up, men dressed down. Because it was near Christmas, some of the women wore sparkling deely-bobbers in their hair, while their men wore Santa Claus hats and thought that was enough to incite roars of laughter.

I was there because I didn't want to be at home alone on a Saturday night. I knew no one. I'd dressed all wrong. What I should have worn was Lurex or leather. To combat the cold, I'd come out in woolly trousers, a man's cardigan over a polo-neck jumper, and my anorak. I kept the lot on because I didn't trust the cloakroom staff. They were tossing the coats just anywhere and getting the ticket slips muddled up with the raffle tickets they were selling.

I watched the dancers, I watched the band. I tapped my plastic beaker of warm white wine with my index finger in time to the beat. But, as the evening wore on, more and more I found myself concentrating, without appearing to, on Karen. My gaze was like a small bird settling for a moment before fluttering away.

After noticing her hair and clothes I'd seen her face. She was lightly tanned. Not a fake, tanning salon tan; more as if she had some Mediterranean blood. I want to say she was cat-like but that's too easy – her nose was thin, a good shape, her mouth was thin, but again a good shape. Her eyes were a brilliant green, slanting and they held me. Setting aside their colour, her eyes appeared shuttered as if nobody was going to read what was going on behind them. This impression was so very definite that it surprised me to see how relaxed the other people at her table were with her, as if they hadn't noticed.

The other tables were all full, most of them reserved by the local retail outlets for their staff Christmas outings. A piece of white card Sellotaped to Karen's table top said: *George's Wine Bars – the place to eat and drink in Sussex.* Everyone seemed to know and like each other. There was a young guy, probably the spoilt baby of the team – he had badly dyed hair, his fringe curling up in the sauna-like heat – then there were eight men and women around Karen's age, generally worn out, downtrodden and tired looking, plus two older guys who looked like maintenance, and an older woman, in her fifties, who might have been a manageress. I put her down as possibly a lesbian. She wore quite a bit of eye makeup, a mustard-coloured, slippery blouse that kept falling off her shoulders, black trousers, sandals, chunky jewellery – would have passed as straight; still, you get to sense these things. A couple of times during the evening she looked over at me and I looked back. Old dyke spots young dyke and assesses. We both broke eye contact at the same time.

Twelve people, thirteen chairs. Everyone trying to be happy and animated except Karen. Everyone in the early stages of getting plastered. The support band shambled off. They'd been useless; a bunch of middle-aged geezers. You get hordes of these in Hastings, incomers who grow what's left of their hair and wear it in a pig's tail of a pigtail. If it sounds as if I despise them, it's not meant to. I see them on the sea front in their too-tight jeans and checked shirts, a battered suede waistcoat hanging open to hide their paunches. Sometimes they stare out at the sea with desperation as if Hastings is their last-chance saloon. Makes me quite emotional behind my dark glasses. Way to go for me yet.

The band was replaced by sounds of the seventies and

eighties: Abba, Blondie, early Madonna. Ricky Martin and Natalie Imbruglia thrown in as a sop to anyone under forty. Then back to the seventies, Hot Chocolate, 'You Sexy Thing'. I groaned silently. Chair occupiers scrambled to their feet. At a table on my left, a middle-aged bloke with a huge beer gut straining his skin-tight tee-shirt simulated sex with one of the deely-bobber women.

I was about to see if the crush at the bar had diminished when a short man in a smart blazer pushed through the heaving crowd. He came round the back of Karen's chair, poked her shoulder, she looked up and he jerked his thumb towards the dance floor. She shook her head. He jerked his thumb again, more insistently. Without looking at anyone, she stood up and followed him. They didn't dance. He held onto her hips and sang the words at her:

"Where did you come from, baby?"

I went to the bar.

I was away some time. The ballroom bar was packed six deep with punters waving tens and twenties. I gave up there and went outside onto the pier, past the bouncers, big blokes in big boots and mega-big overcoats.

"You had your hand stamped?"

I held up the back of my hand.

Going outside doesn't mean you are outside on Hastings pier. It's not that easy. Poky shops have been built facing each other, under cover, sort of a tunnel of shops. Without the lighting the tunnel's dark, and even with lighting it's not a cheerful place to be. Hippy shops selling candles, ethnic and crushed velvet, a nail bar, a musical instrument kiosk, empty carcasses – dark inside with broken boxes and scraps of paper on the floor left by the last occupier. It's all poverty trying to look colourful and bohemian. At home I've got stacks of candles because I feel so sorry for the woman in the candle shop, sitting in her big jumper and fingerless gloves trying not to shiver.

I found the Pub on the Pier. Shabby's good in a pub. I waited ten minutes to be served. I didn't mind – at least the temperature was near normal; my feet warmed up, my body cooled down.

I forgot about Karen. It was still the start of the evening, only ten o'clock, my interest at that point could have disappeared if I'd seen better. I bought a pint of white wine for later and a whisky to warm me up and took my drinks to an empty table. Plenty of overspill from the dance. There were groups of women with faces like carefully prepared masks; dyed hair sprayed into shape – not even a gale would have shifted their fringes. Nearly all of them had the ferocious fake tans that made their skin look pockmarked under the harsh pub lighting. I picked out the ones who went to the gym. They were thin with good muscle tone in their upper arms. The ones who didn't go to any gym – the flabby ones wearing distracting chiffon scarves and flashing gob-stopping earrings. And the ones who didn't need a gym – the younger girls, the shiny, straight-haired girls with skin like rose petals. The men, I took no notice of. I registered them, that was all: loud voices, *fahking* this, *fahking* that, *stupid cahnt!*

Whisky finished, I thought of Karen and how her face had been while the blazer was grinding and singing. Resigned. Removed.

Carrying my pint of wine, I left the pub and returned to my station in front of the fire door. The dance floor was emptying. Nobody was ready to slow the tempo down for 'California Dreaming'. It was too early. Karen and the blazer were returning to their table. He walked ahead of her. He went to the chair next to the one she'd been sitting on. Karen peeled off and took an empty chair further round the table. He gave her a hard stare. She kept her head down. While they'd been away someone had refilled the glasses and she grabbed hers and knocked back the contents as if she was dying of thirst and vodka was no stronger than water. She turned her attention to the older, dykey woman.

I'll tell you a bit about the blazer. He must have been fifty, short, and stockily built. His head was bullet shaped, emphasised by the close cut of his vigorous, iron-grey hair. He wore polished, slip-on shoes and grey trousers, a blinding white shirt under the blazer and a club tie. Old fashioned in that way rich blokes can get away with. The others at the table were polite but not really at ease with him, which made me think he must be their boss.

Karen was getting drunker quicker than anyone. I noted a protective tenderness amongst the rest of them. The drunker she got, the more vulnerable she seemed. The blazer couldn't keep his eyes off her. No tenderness there, more like hunger.

Time passed. People went walkabout. The closely held boundaries of each party began to merge. The bloke with the beer gut asked Karen to dance. When she stood up, she was a head taller than he was, her breasts coming just below his chin. She laughed. He buried his face in her breasts, grabbing hold and wobbling them against his cheeks while she stared over his bent head with a vacant expression on her face as if this was just routine and let him get on with it. The older woman (I'll call her the manageress) stood up. With great good humour, she inserted her arm between Karen's breasts and the bloke's face so he had to step back. As he did so, the manageress latched onto his shoulders and smoothly drew him out onto the dance floor. The blazer was on his feet. He took hold of Karen's arm and shook it. "What the fuck do you think you're up to? Well?"

"Well what?"

She brushed his hand off her arm like she was brushing away a speck of dirt and sat down. Before he could reach the next chair, the manageress was back and sitting in it.

About that time I started to take more notice of the manageress. I put her down as Karen's protectress and began rooting for her as if she and the blazer were in a race, with Karen for the prize. She had short hair and a smoker's face; angular and lined. She didn't look as if she'd ever been happy, because the lines on her face had all settled, going in the one direction – downwards. She'd positioned herself sideways so Karen could lean back against her. After a while she casually draped an arm around Karen's shoulders. With her free hand she lit a fag, pulling on it before gently putting it between Karen's lips. They were like two people who'd just enjoyed good sex together.

The night should have been interminable. It wasn't, it shot past. Each time I glanced at my watch another big segment of time had ticked away: ten, eleven, midnight. The main band was due on. The deely-bobber women came over to the George's Wine Bars table and asked if someone would keep an eye on their handbags while they went out for chips. The blazer said, "Bring us back some chips and we might think about it."

"Of course we'll keep an eye on your bags," the manageress said.

"I'm serious about those chips," said the blazer.

"Anyone else for chips?" the deely-bobbers asked.

No one else for chips. The manageress went out on the dance floor on her own, giving all she'd got to Bonnie Tyler's 'Holding out for a Hero'.

"Where have all the good men gone

And where are all the gods?"

Her eyes were shut and she looked as if she needed no one.

Back at the table the blazer was eating chips from a Styrofoam carton. At one point he leant across the table and offered Karen his fingers to lick. She knocked his hand away. He came back at her, pushing his middle finger at her mouth.

"Isn't there a white knight on a fiery steed?"

Each way her face turned, his fat, greasy middle finger followed.

"And he's got to be sure and he's got to be soon

and he's got to be larger than life..."

Karen unsteadily scraped her chair round to face the dancers. With a laugh he sat back, took out a white handkerchief and wiped his hands.

What next? The raffle followed by the main band. The minor celebrity playing Snow White in the pantomime across the road had been booked to announce the winners, but she got waylaid by fans at the bar, so the organisers hauled someone's granny on stage, who was celebrating her fiftieth wedding anniversary even though hubby had been dead for fourteen years. Everyone cheered. Women shouted, "Aahh!" and looked at each other as if that must be the sublime outcome to a perfect life.

As raffles went, it was a good raffle. The ticket holders got really excited. I saw a foot spa, a giant Body Shop basket, and a six pack of Asti Spumante being carried past me to the deely-bobber table. The George's Wine Bars hadn't bothered to buy raffle tickets so they all looked bored. The manageress went off with one of the older guys to get more drinks. Snow White was found. There was a general cheer until she tried to talk about the pantomime running for another ten days and how the tickets were ten pounds – twelve pounds for the circle – with special rates for children. She had a high, piping voice, which was fine for being Snow White but useless getting heard over a drunken crowd.

Someone yelled, "Piss off now, darling," and lobbed a plastic cup.

Twelve-thirty. The ballroom lights dimmed, the stage lights switched off. There was a drum roll while smoke from dry ice seeped across the stage. Red spots drilled the smoke. Eight blokes ran on stage, two of them wearing hats and sun glasses to look like the Blues Brothers. That was the only resemblance.

"Do you want to rock?" they shouted.

"Yes," we shouted back.

"DO YOU WANT TO ROCK?"

"YEAH!"

"THEN LET'S ROCK!" and they creaked into 'Jumping Jack Flash'.

Everybody was up on their feet, all the tables emptying. I watched faces. The crowd was transformed, imagining themselves young Mick Jaggers or young Mick Jagger's girlies. Karen climbed unsteadily onto a chair. She pulled up her shirt and tucked the ends into her bra, then began an inept belly-dancing routine. From the crowd she picked out a bloke who looked a bit like the actor, Alfred Molina. He'd won a four-foot-high teddy bear in the raffle and seemed happy to dance with it for the rest of the evening. Alfred had a nice face. I put him down as middle management in a caring, sharing building society. He held teddy in front of him and worked teddy's arms so they waved at Karen and in return she undulated her whole body and made sexy passes in the air for teddy's benefit. Everyone was laughing. It looked innocent and funny. Then she fell off the chair. Not gracefully – the chair tipped up and her leather-clad legs shot up in the air as her bum hit the ground. Alfred and his teddy bear rushed over to help her up. She was ok – laughing and rubbing her backside.

He got her to her feet and she fell forward into teddy's arms, resting her head on the bear's shoulder while slipping her hands under Alfred's jacket. Alfred looked pleasantly bewildered but too drunk to really engage properly with what she was doing. At this point the blazer, who was the only one left at their table, got to his feet and marched over. He didn't seem annoyed or jealous... he looked as if he was quite unemotionally retrieving his personal property. He peeled her away from man and bear, led her back to the table and sat her down. He sat next to her.

She wouldn't look at him. He stared at her averted profile. He put one hand on his knee and the other on Karen's knee. His head was as close to her face as he could get it. Her expression was blank as if she'd cut him and everything else out. Suddenly she noticed that the buttons of her shirt were undone to below her bra – you could see nearly all of her breasts. With difficulty she did up two buttons. It took her ages to get button through button hole. All this time he continued talking steadily to her, although I don't know how she could hear because the music was so loud. I counted 'Rockin' all Over the World', 'Love is the Drug' and 'Nutbush City Limits' and still he kept on talking. At one point she held out her hands, palms up, against him, like she was pushing his words away. I noticed her nails; they were false, long, squared off and painted silver with a tiny diamond above each cuticle.

By then I'd moved nearer, stood at the edge of their table, rocking slightly to maintain my balance. I was very drunk. My circle of awareness had reduced to Karen and Mister Blazer, Mister Bullet Head, Mister In-your-face Intrusive.

Karen jerked her chin up as if she was trying to keep her head above water, her eyes everywhere searching for... blue sky, a hero? All I needed was one look, a plea to step in. I rehearsed the words, "Is he bothering you? Are you ok? Nobody owns you."

I looked into her eyes. No I can't exactly say I looked into her eyes because her eyes wouldn't be looked into – nowhere in her face did I read a plea for help. Her head tipped higher and higher to get it out of his range while he kept on rabbiting.

I searched the crowd for the manageress. There she was, part of a circle dancing to the band's lousy rendition of 'Brown Girl in the Ring'. They were all singing along. Even the manageress was singing though she seemed too world weary to relish a sing-song. She didn't look happy. None of them in the circle looked that happy. Nothing like the deely-bobber crowd who were so happy they might start fighting soon.

The blazer took hold of Karen's wrist and yanked her to her feet. He pulled her towards his all-dancing, all-singing, unhappy staff. They broke the circle and let the two of them in. The manageress was on one side of Karen, the blazer on the other. The manageress took her hand while he kept his grip on her wrist. Between them they stopped her from falling or from just slipping down onto the floor. Karen didn't really dance, she jerked about like a badly controlled puppet. Her shirt had ridden up and there were glimpses of white fleshy stomach. I sat at their empty table, in the seat Karen had just vacated. I drank what remained of the vodka in her plastic glass. Now there was no sign of Karen or the blazer or the manageress, they'd gone deep onto the dance floor. I saw Alfred Molina with his teddy bear. He looked well pleased with the bear as if he'd found a true friend. He saw me watching him and he grinned, lifted the bear's paw and waved it at me. I waved back.

A Slice of Melon

When Kelly said, "Fancy a shag?", Laura replied, "Don't mind if I do," which seemed to satisfy Kelly, although Laura wasn't too happy with her own choice of words. *Don't mind if I do* was what Norma Next Door said to offers of tea, cake, Pringles, and Bacardi and Coke. Fortunately Kelly didn't know Norma Next Door.

When Laura was fifteen she'd had – well, she couldn't call it sex or a shag – she'd had 'something' with Norma Next Door, who was eighteen and had recently become engaged to Rick, a deliverer of organic potatoes.

"I want to show you this thing Rick does to me. It drives me wild," Norma said. "It's instead of going the whole way. Rick wants to wait till we're married. Rick says holding back will increase our levels of sexual pleasure."

"But I'm not a man," Laura protested.

"You don't have to be, stupid. You've got the same hair as Rick though, short and stubbly."

She took Laura into her kitchen and behind a wooden clothes horse, hung with her dad's vests and impressive Y-fronts.

"Just sit on the floor."

Laura sat and watched Norma take off her knickers. Through the wall she heard the *Archers* theme tune. Her mum would be laying the table and looking at the clock to see if it was indeed five past seven.

"I want you to put your head between my legs," Norma said, standing with her legs wide apart.

"I don't know that I want to."

"But I want you to."

"I want to know what's going to happen, first."

"I'm going to come on the top of your head," Norma said.

"You are not." Laura rubbed the top of her head vigorously.

"Don't worry. I'll do something back to you."

"What?"

"Something. A surprise. Wait and see."

It hadn't been as straightforward as Norma coming on Laura's head. Laura had to advance the top of her head slowly up Norma's short skirt, so that her spiky hair only brushed Norma's vaginal lips, then retreat, then advance again. Retreat. Then advance again.

"Ugh, ugh," Norma kept repeating, "Your little head. Your little, little head."

It was quite exciting, tantalising Norma, until the moment when Norma locked Laura's head in the vice of her thighs and began to bear down hard, then to the right, then to the left, then in a circular movement. At one point Laura saw stars, imagined herself with a broken neck. Would it be considered murder, manslaughter or a crime of passion? Would it only come under the heading of 'an accident in the home'?

"Oh ye-es," Norma said, ingesting Laura's head almost to her eyebrows.

"My turn now," Laura said.

"Sit down."

"I am sitting down."

"Like this," and she pushed Laura back till her head and shoulders leant against the seat of an armchair. Then she positioned the clothes horse so that the struts fell each side of Laura's neck. Three pairs of Y-fronts hung between them.

"You part your legs like this."

"Shouldn't I take my jeans off?"

"Better not. Dad might walk in at any minute. I'll just undo your zip and ease them down." Laura felt the cool air caress her bare thighs.

"Ready?"

"Yes."

"Ok." Norma's fingers began to trace circles on Laura's skin. Laura shivered with expectation.

"Round and round the garden like a teddy bear, one step, two steps, and a tickly under there," Norma recited, then scrabbled on the outside of Laura's knickers.

Three times she did this before stopping. Laura heard her stand up, then Norma's hand appeared, scrunching a pair of underpants. "These are dry," she said.

Now Laura was nearly eighteen, and everyone (herself included) agreed that she was young for her age. Laura blamed her lack of cash and a widowed mother who was interested in every facet of her daughter's life as long as it was a facet similar to her own facets. Dreary facets, problematic facets and sexual diversity facets had to be concealed, could not be discussed. If a television programme came on that could in any way further Laura's limited sexual knowledge, her mother turned the sound right down and began talking loudly.

Laura felt she had the general idea of what a shag with Kelly involved, but wasn't absolutely clear on the fine detail. Had she been able to order the *The Bumper Book of Lesbian Sex: A photographic manual*, from the Libertas website, she'd have felt more confident, but it seemed bumper books were for wage earners rather than sixth formers, as it was seventeen pounds nineteen pence plus postage and packing. And then there was the difficulty of intercepting the postman and getting the package past her mother, who always hung about the hall in the morning in expectation of a letter to say she'd won the Premium Bonds, which happened surprisingly often.

"Only the *Works of Shakespeare*, Mum."

"Really darling, how fascinating. Does it include the Sonnets? Let's see if I can find 'Those lips that Love's own hand did make'. Your dad used to quote that whenever we had an argument..."

"Just the *New English Bible*, Mum."

"I haven't seen a copy of the Bible in years. I bet they've made a hash of the Sermon on the Mount."

Kelly had been in the year above Laura but was now taking a gap year before going to Brighton University. She wore black jeans and black tee-shirts always. She was wiry with short, light brown hair. Had long hands and feet. Laura had watched her in the school gym doing handstands and cartwheels at a slow and thoughtful pace. With such hands and feet, it seemed possible that Kelly was capable of being a world-famous pianist, a surgeon, or at least an Olympic athlete. Laura particularly admired her ability to never smile.

Kelly lived with her mum and older sister in a flat in Stoke Newington.

"They'll be at work," she said. "Place to ourselves."

Laura liked words but Kelly used only those necessary to make herself understood, which Laura again found admirable and a goal worth aspiring to in her own life. She wondered why Kelly had chosen her. Where Kelly's confidence came from.

They arranged to meet on Tuesday during her school lunch

hour, which was actually one hour and three quarters now she was in the sixth form.

A date. My first date. She'd have liked to tell somebody, but at school she'd already told everyone she'd been dating for years. She'd said boys as well as girls. Actually she'd said, "Male and female," which she thought sounded more sophisticated. She'd told Mum there was plenty of time for boys when she finished her 'A' levels.

"Good girl," Mum said, "You've got your whole life ahead of you."

Laura walked through Ridley Road Market looking at the stalls, wondering if a melon would be a cool thing to take or rubbish. It was the most sensual fruit she could see: taut, glossy green skin, some of them sliced open to reveal a glisteningly moist pink inside. She and Kelly could slice theirs open. Well, Kelly could slice it open as it was her flat and Laura didn't want to seem presumptuous foraging for a sharp knife and a large plate. Carry several of the slices to Kelly's bedroom. Later, on the bed, the juice dripping from their chins, making snail trails over their bare breasts and hanging like teardrops from their nipples. Now, why had she come up with snail trails? That wasn't an erotic image at all. But the path of the juice would look like that – or slug trails. Better to stick to snails. Snails could be considered cute if one wasn't a gardener. She couldn't imagine Kelly gardening. What could she imagine Kelly doing? She bought the melon.

Nobody gardened; that was obvious. Laura stepped over two bikes sprawling on the path. Instead of garden there was a square of cracked concrete and three black dustbins with 27 A, B and C daubed on the lids in white paint. Kelly opened the front door as she put her foot on the first step of five. Good sign. She must have been watching from a window.

"Hi," Laura said.

"What's that?"

"A melon. I thought it was a sexy fruit."

"Sexy?"

Laura reddened. "Well, erotic."

"Erotic?" Kelly stepped sideways to let Laura into the hall. "Go right to the top," she said.

Right to the top was up three flights. The stair carpet disappeared.

"Floor sanded," Kelly said.

"That's great."

"Yeah? How great? Pink door."

The brass doorknob came off in Laura's hand.

"Push not pull," Kelly said, taking it from her.

Laura went in; Kelly came in fast behind her and kicked the door shut. At first all Laura could see was shrouded shapes. The blind was pulled down, shutting out the light.

Laura fumbled for a light switch.

"Don't," Kelly said, "Don't move."

She lit a candle, then another. There were no shrouded shapes, just a double bed, a rail of clothes, a tailor's dummy wearing a dinner jacket and silk scarf, plus a narrow bookcase crammed with paperbacks. The bed was covered in a velvet patchwork of wine, green, blue and black. On the floor next to the bed was a white long-haired rug.

"Argos," Kelly said, seeing Laura looking at it.

Above the bed hung a drawing of a nude woman lying against a patchwork background.

"That's brilliant," Laura said.

"Sit. Lie. Don't stand." Kelly threw herself on the bed.

Laura sat. "Did you draw that?"

"Yes."

"Did she go to our school?"

"She's a mate of Mum's."

"Did you sleep with her?"

"Yes."

Laura put the melon down between them. On a television programme she'd seen, women were advised to sensuously draw attention to their faces... she touched her cheek then traced her top lip with her index finger... T*hose lips that Love's own hand did make...* go away, Shakespeare's sonnet... which reminded her of Mum and on to Dad when he was really ill, still wolf-whistling at Mum. Concentrate. She moistened her index finger on her moist bottom lip, caressed the line of jaw, her hand gliding down her neck to the V of whatever she was wearing... only in this instance there was no V, just the round neck of Laura's bottle-green school sweatshirt.

"Drink?"

"Like what?"

"Wine?"

In seventy-five minutes, English Literature. "Better not," Laura said. "We could have a slice of this. It's very refreshing."

By the flickering light of the candles, Laura couldn't swear that Kelly smiled, but certainly some lighter expression passed across her face.

"Back in a minute. Get undressed."

Quickly Laura took off her clothes, draping them neatly over the rail. There was no mirror, which was a pity. She'd have liked to reassure herself that her figure was ok, her breasts were her best feature and that her face looked attractive by candle light. She considered lounging back on the bed to imitate the pose of the woman in the picture, but the woman's hair was black and long enough to coil around one breast while Laura's hair was cropped and a silky blonde. Self-consciously, she sat on the velvet bedspread. How to sit seductively without inspiring derision? Tried one leg stretched out, the other bent, both hands holding the bent leg's ankle – too much like a yoga position, which was fine if Kelly knew as little about yoga as she did, but not fine if Kelly knew a lot about yoga and thought Laura was pretending to be... a yogi? Where was Kelly?

Glanced at Kelly's bookcase: *Prozac Highway, Stone Butch Blues, Fingersmith, Rubyfruit...* so many books that Laura had heard of but never read. Did Kelly lend out her books? Where *was* Kelly? Better lie down and look... seductive, voluptuous. Her breasts were definitely voluptuous.

Turned down the bedspread. Put a pillow behind her head. Stretched out her legs and crossed them at the ankles. Perfectly relaxed. Looked down between her voluptuous breasts and saw tufts of her darker pubic hair like the crowns of distant trees showing above a gentle hillside. Tiny distant trees above a gentle sand dune would be more accurate. Should she fluff the trees up a little or were they better sleeked down? Up? Or down? She brushed her pubic hair with the side of her hand.

"What are you doing?" Kelly asked, quite pleasantly, standing in the doorway. She wore a black silk kimono and carried a plate on which two slices of melon lay.

"Waiting for you," Laura said. Realising that staring down through her breasts gave her at least three chins, she rolled on her side and patted the bed invitingly.

Kelly sat down on the bed. The front of the kimono fell open. There was the curved shadow of her breast. Like a scimitar, Laura thought. Automatically, she clenched the top of her thighs. *Make this not be a disappointment.*

They each took a slice of melon. It was almost exactly how Laura had imagined it. The juice spurted into her mouth, up her nostrils, ran down her chin, made snail trails over her breasts and hung like teardrops from her nipples. Kelly put her own slice back on the plate and caught each teardrop in her mouth. Her tongue flicked over Laura's nipple, her hand squeezed Laura's other breast. Laura stroked Kelly's hair, the back of Kelly's neck, over the silk cloth covering her shoulder and down towards the opening of the kimono.

She thought she imagined it, an involuntary intake of breath from Kelly. Kelly took Laura's hands and eased her back against the pillows, parted her legs and knelt between them. The thought left Laura's head. For the first time in her life she was focused. Shagging – wrong word. Fucking – wrong word. Softer, harder. Kelly kissing her breasts, her stomach, sliding in her fingers, two, three, four. Laura squirming, desperate. Face wet. Hair roots steaming. Kelly watching her face intently. *Something not right... not right... not right.* The voice fading as her excitement built.

She reached out to Kelly. "Let me touch you," she gasped, pulling at the kimono sash.

"Leave it," Kelly's voice sharp, almost... what was the note? Fear?

"Please." Laura eased herself up on one elbow and reached for the soft weight of Kelly's breast beneath the cloth.

Kelly took her hand firmly and laid it on the bed next to the plate.

"No," she said, "don't spoil it."

Which spoilt it. Laura's excitement didn't die. It became secondary. She turned her inner eye on herself, lying with her legs open, her skin flushed and damp, sweat gathered in the hollow of her neck and beneath her eyes, and then out towards Kelly, her body almost completely concealed, her portion of melon untouched.

"Why?" she asked, her legs closing like a flower as the sun disappears.

"I get my excitement from watching you," Kelly said. For her, a comparatively long sentence.

"But that's not... the whole of it."

"What do you know?" Kelly slipped from between her legs and stood up.

"I know that's not enough for me," Laura said. "I feel like your victim."

"I withdraw," Kelly said, tying her sash more securely.

"Pardon? What?" Laura said startled. "You withdraw? What does that mean?"

"I'm withdrawing from the shag," she said, picking up the plate with its one whole slice of melon, one smiling segment of rind. "I'll let you get dressed."

"Is that it?"

"Seems to be." And she left the bedroom.

Laura put on her clothes painfully, cramps in her stomach, ache in her heart, her mind confused, hurt, embarrassed, angry. For a moment she looked at the picture above the bed. Had Kelly been enough for her? She thought of Norma Next Door. Was this to be her sexual portion, women always doing what they wanted and never mind about what she wanted?

Kelly sat at the kitchen table. She'd cut the flesh from her slice of melon and was eating it with a fork. She didn't look up.

Laura said, "I really liked you. I thought you were special. In a way I still think you're special."

Then Kelly looked up. She looks much more than a year older than me, Laura thought, and not happy. Or confident.

"You'll know what to expect next time," Kelly said.

"What do you mean?"

"The next time I ask you if you fancy a shag."

"So there will be a next time?"

"If you want."

"If you want."

"Whatever. Thanks for this." She speared another chunk of melon.

Laura sat through English Literature thinking. What would she say if Kelly asked her again?

"You must be joking. In your dreams!"

No, she would say yes. Probably say, "Don't mind if I do," and spend the next hour regretting it. Follow it through to the end next time, because...? Kelly could do cartwheels and handstands, owned books she'd like to read, could draw, had a mother whose friends posed nude and had sex with their friends' daughters. Because Kelly was – not a million times, that would be ridiculous – but at least a hundred times more interesting and... complex, than she'd expected her to be. Vulnerable as well. She'd certainly detected vulnerability.

Laura felt better. As her father used to say (admittedly about Arsenal), 'It was a result.' She felt a light tap on her shoulder. Miss Mayhew, the English teacher, stood over her, making passes in the air with a clear plastic ruler.

"Are you with us, Laura?"

Laura resisted replying, "I'm with the Woolwich," which would have got a cheap laugh but was a very old joke and one she'd rather not be associated with.

Instead she said, "I'm sorry, I was daydreaming."

"Fair enough," Miss Mayhew said, "I don't blame you."

Miss Mayhew was an attractive woman in her early twenties who wore knotted string ties. The other students reckoned Laura was her favourite. They were right.

Maria's Mother

"The simple explanation of memory is that a sensation washes through the brain leaving behind a residue of neural connections. When this group of nerves are prompted to fire together, they begin to sprout fine, threadlike processes called dendrites. In this way, a fleeting sensation can leave a permanent pattern of connections embedded in the brain. Having been created, this web of connections will lie dormant and unnoticed..." McCrone, 1996

My name is Stephanie. I am a youngish woman who looks older. Maria, my dearest friend and life partner, is a young woman still. I'm a journalist who makes her living writing semi-revelatory medical articles for women's magazines: 'The truth about anti-depressants', 'Are you a secret pill junkie?' Sometimes an interesting, oddball piece crops up in the *New Scientist* or the *Lancet* which makes good copy. I've become well respected, almost as if I've done the research myself.

This is mine and Maria's story. Unfortunately not a romance. Had I started writing a couple of years ago, it would have been romantic if uneventful. No, this is a much better story for those outside looking in. Our friends are curious. They know something is wrong. They scent tragedy.

Going back. One of Maria's many attractions was her abundant energy. She was never half-hearted. Her absolute enthusiastic commitment was endearing to someone like me who is intrinsically... lazy. This energy of Maria's manifested itself in her mobile, vivacious face, the vigorous health of her dark, curly hair and strong, slender limbs that were rarely still. She ate healthily, worked, swam, played volleyball and rounders. I look wistfully into our past and see only a blur of movement that is Maria.

Last summer, it was very hot. When Maria complained of tiredness, I wasn't worried. She said it was nothing like exhaustion, more a languorous desire to let her eyes sleep. Particularly her left eye. The first visible evidence that anything was seriously wrong was when the reddened white of her eye and a slight drooping of the lid surprised her from the bathroom mirror.

"Too many late nights," was her conclusion. "Your bloody cigarette smoke. Maybe I'm just run down."

I promised to keep to my promise of smoking outside. The next day, at lunchtime, Maria went to Boots, where the assistant recommended eye drops. Two in both eyes, if the problem persisted, see a doctor.

"I think a little better," Maria said that evening.

"Much better," I said, "you look beautiful."

I remember now that Maria frowned. Fleetingly.

During the night I had to wake her by shaking her shoulder. The ear-splitting whining sound she was making in her sleep was unnerving.

"Maria, please. Stop it," I said quite sharply.

It took her a moment to wake properly. I switched on the bedside lamp. Immediately our bedroom looked warm and secure.

"I'm sorry," I said, "but you woke me out of a very pleasant dream."

"Stephanie, my head aches," she said like a child, raising her left hand to the left side of her forehead.

"I'll get you a couple of paracetemols."

"Codeine."

"What?"

"Codeine. That's what Mum used to take."

"But that was years ago. You'll have to make do with paracetemols."

"In large brown bottles. I remember them. Can I see the bottle?"

"Of course not. These come in a packet. You know they do. Don't you? Maria, open both your eyes."

With difficulty her left lid rose. The white was red again but also the surrounding skin looked purplish. The eye didn't engage with mine like the right one did. As if the thinking that governed it had altered. I felt chilled. I went into the kitchen and found paracetemol and a glass of water. By the time I reached the bedroom, Maria was fast asleep and breathing normally. Her left arm was flung across her eyes. I swallowed both pills, drank a few sips of water before getting back into bed. I put out the light. For some time I lay awake imagining Maria's left eye, imagining it was still slightly open in the shadow of her arm.

Two years ago I met Maria's mother for the first time. Maria had no idea who her father was. He could have been one of any number of men. In the seventies and eighties, her mother had been promiscuous, men passing through her home like trains stopping briefly at a station.

"Did the men make her happy?" I'd asked.

"I think so. That was how she liked men to be – never staying long. She didn't want to tire of them or them to tire of her."

"These men never tried anything on with you?" I'd asked, anger stirring in my chest.

She shook her head. "She kept being a mother separate from her own needs."

I hadn't been impressed.

Maria's mother had breast cancer and was due to go into hospital. I wasn't keen to meet her. The little Maria had told me had produced a mental image of a clapped-out... Well, I hold up my hands: yes, I know mothers are women in their own right, but I couldn't bear the thought of my Maria as a child with frantic sexual activity going on in another room. Her mother with a comparative stranger. And again. And again.

We set off to visit her on a sunny autumn morning. I drove, Maria directed. Finally we came to a miserable kind of urban countryside running along part of the east coast. I couldn't imagine Maria growing up in such a dreary area.

"Down here," she said, directing me into a lane.

Above the car, the trees formed an orange and yellow canopy. We seemed to be driving through a wood. Not a sign of habitation on either side.

"Slow down. We're nearly there."

"Are we? I can't see a house." And then I saw a wooden sign nailed to a tree trunk: Fern Lodge. We drove a further fifty yards before reaching a small clearing.

"Is this it?"

"Yes," she said almost impatiently.

I turned the car, the wheels crunching over stony soil and small fallen branches. We were on little more than a cart track. How the devil had Maria's mother's lovers managed to find their way here after dark? Suddenly the trees fell away and we emerged into sunlight. In front of us stood a house, colonial style with a wooden veranda running the full width, with steps leading down to the garden.

"Park next to Mum's car," Maria said, nodding at a blue Astra. I pulled in, noting that the roof and bonnet of the Astra were covered with leaves and a coating of dust as if it hadn't been moved in some time.

No sign of Maria's mother. Nobody throwing open the porch door and calling out a welcome. We got out of the car and I followed Maria across the grass. I'd have liked to hold her hand, presented a united loving front – god knows for what reason, as Maria had told her mother about preferring women to men when she was still in her early teens.

Leaves fluttered from the trees like gold feathers. In the air was a lovely smell: fresh air, wet foliage and wood smoke. I looked up and sure enough, a line of grey smoke rose from the house's chimney. In an upstairs window I saw a curtain move. We climbed the steps to the veranda. I had a fleeting thought, "This would be a wonderful place to live," and then the door opened.

"Hello," Maria's mother said.

She was young. I don't mean well preserved. She looked like a young woman, although she was fifty-eight. Late middle-age. Maria will be like that. Which didn't mean that I liked Maria's mother, because I didn't. In fact, I liked her even less than I'd expected to. The leathery, hard-bitten, nymphomaniac of my imagination would almost have been preferable. Easier. I could have felt pity. She would have reinforced some puritanical ethos of my own. This young-looking woman was a threat.

She kissed my cheek. She smelt like Maria. I didn't quite jerk my head away but she felt my recoil because she stepped back and surveyed me with an amused smile.

"Sit down," she said. "We'll have lunch out here. I think it's warm enough."

There was a wooden table and four faded cane chairs. I sat.

"Enjoy my view," Maria's mother said. She threw the words back over her shoulder as she followed Maria indoors. I had the disturbing sense of sitting where so many men had sat before, all being told to enjoy her view while she fixed them something to eat, or drink, or fixed herself.

When they brought out the food I got to my feet. I said, "Let me –" but, with a movement of her hip, Maria's mother eased the table against me so I was forced back into my chair.

The meal was simple: salad, French bread, a variety of cheeses, white wine – a Muscadet. I was driving, so hardly touched my glass. Between them they finished the bottle. I didn't put much into the conversation, I watched them. They were like birds of the same species. In comparison, I felt like an elderly, grizzled badger, a creature of the earth, head down, unnoticed, while the birds sang above me.

"You're very quiet, Steph," Maria's mother said at last while Maria was inside making coffee.

Automatically I corrected her, "Stephanie."

She smiled, tipping her face sideways, her chin resting on the back of her left hand. For a second she looked just like my Maria.

"Stephanie sounds very feminine. I prefer Steph," she said.

For the first time our eyes locked and what I read in hers was hostility. I felt a flicker of surprise. I kept my voice reasonable and good humoured. "I'm not a feminine woman but I am a woman," I said and smiled back at her.

"As you walked towards the house I could almost have mistaken you for a man." She paused and made a sad little sound which I knew was meant to come out as a pretty laugh. "I expect Maria's told you how much I... value men."

"Yes," I replied gently, "but you won't mind if Maria values me?"

She folded her hands in her lap. For that moment I felt all the emotions I should have felt for a woman possibly dying of cancer: pity, sorrow, affection, understanding – she looked so dreadfully lost.

"You'll do," she said.

Before we left, Maria showed me her childhood bedroom. She led me up a flight of wooden stairs to a room in the roof not visible from the garden. It was large and airy, brightly coloured rugs on the floorboards, a single bed painted white, still made up as if the child Maria was expected back at any moment. I walked across to the big dormer window and gasped. Below was the edge of a cliff and then there was the sea, glittering under the late afternoon sun.

"I had no idea we were so near the coast," I said.

Maria put her arms around my waist. "Me and Mum used to swim every day for most of the year."

"You never told me."

"You never asked. You know I like swimming."

"You like every sport there is."

"But particularly swimming. Mum's the same. She's like a fish. We're a fishy little family."

I woke heavy headed from the paracetemols and disturbed night. Maria was still asleep, which was unusual. I let her sleep while I gathered up some notes for an article I was researching in the British Library. As I switched the kettle on, I heard her stirring. I made us both a cup of tea. I thought about picking a rosebud from the garden. It's the kind of romantic gesture I made from time to time, but outside there was a fine drizzle so I left that idea for another morning.

Maria was sitting up against a heap of pillows. Her left eye was back to normal, not the slightest trace of reddening.

"How are you feeling?" I asked, putting the tea down on the bedside table.

"Better. I'm sorry I woke you up in the night."

"I was quite worried. You asked for codeine. Said something about your mother and a brown bottle of codeine."

"I don't remember. Funnily enough I was dreaming about her..." She frowned as she tried to recall her dream and, as she did so, her left eyelid drooped slightly. It looked quite bizarre, as if someone – not Maria, but someone – was winking at me.

"Don't do that," I said sharply.

Surprised, she looked up. "Don't do what?"

"You were letting your eyelid droop."

"Was I? Pass me the mirror."

"Look, it's fine. I'm just jittery. I'm never any good when I've not had my full eight hours."

"Please," she wheedled, "I want to see."

I passed over her hand mirror and she studied her reflection. "At least my eye's not bloodshot any more. But you're right, I think there is a problem with that eyelid. I'm going to make an appointment with the doctor."

I said, "I don't think there's any need for that."

I didn't say it with any real conviction. I wanted her to go.

"You're probably right," she said, "I'll leave it for now. I hate doctors."

"... the words we learn and the networks of meaning which become attached to them, also texture our brain circuitry. In simple terms,

they carve out memory paths that would not otherwise be present in our heads..."

That evening I got home about six. I was tired. The Piccadilly line had seemed even stuffier and more crowded than usual. I unlocked the front door and let the house work its magic. From where I stood in the hall I could see the kitchen table: on it a blue vase decorated with dark-feathered kingfishers, a flash of colour on their breasts and beaks. Maria had filled it with cornflowers and foliage from our eucalyptus tree.

"Maria!" I called out. No answer. I listened. From upstairs I heard the slight but distinct creak of a floorboard, which meant Maria was in the box room. I didn't go up immediately. I took off my jacket and draped it over the back of a kitchen chair. I switched the kettle on, shouting out, "Maria!" again. Still she didn't answer me. I started up the stairs. Before I'd gone even halfway, the same high-pitched whining sound of the night before started above me. This time there was an angry quality to it, like it was warning an enemy to take care. Come no closer. I hesitated. I could see the door of the box room. It was ajar and then suddenly it clicked shut.

I told myself, it's only Maria, but I was spooked. My heart beat faster.

Our box room is literally a box-shaped room in which we keep boxes full of my medical journals, magazines, case histories and newspaper cuttings I no longer need but might want for reference one day. Maria had been glad to see my stuff packed up and the door closed on it. She'd said, half-seriously, that this was our home and these articles of mine chronicling other people's misery created small areas of unsafety in the house.

Before I'd used the room for storage, we'd been saving it,

hoping that one day Maria would have a child and it would become a nursery. For three years we put all our energies and money into Maria conceiving. We became obsessive: the visits to the different clinics, the doctors, money spent – hope, false hope, no hope at all. We came close to a real argument. I wanted that child. I felt it was nearby, waiting to be born. I could stretch out my hand, the child could stretch out its hand. Our fingers could almost touch.

It was Maria who finally said, "Enough." She was – still is – a woman of graceful movements but on that morning she struck an untypically awkward pose, like a street fighter, her arms bent and raised as if she was about to go for me with her clenched fists, her soft, pretty face set into hard angles, her eyes dangerous.

I said, "Calm down. You're right, nothing really matters apart from the two of us. Ok, this stops now."

As I turned the brass doorknob to the box room, the whining sound abruptly ceased. For some foolish reason I'd expected to have difficulty getting the door open. I imagined an altered Maria on the other side trying to keep me out, but no, the door swung easily back. The room was full of sunlight. Maria stood in front of the small window that looked out over the neighbourhood gardens. Around her were several open boxes. She appeared neither strange nor defiant, or in any way like a woman who up till five seconds earlier had been keening in such a bloodchilling way. This was just my Maria, completely normal, looking up at me, her face as clear and open as it always was.

"I wanted one of the old photograph albums," she said.

"You won't find them up here. They're downstairs in the leather trunk. This is all my stuff. Nothing of yours or ours."

"That explains it," she said. Briskly, she brushed her right forearm with her left hand. I experienced the unsettling sensation that her left hand was admonishing that right forearm.

Now, what was going on in my head that I said absolutely nothing? I didn't ask her why she hadn't answered when I'd called, why she'd shut the door as I came up the stairs and why she'd been making such an unholy noise. I waited for her to say something to release me from my silence. She didn't. The weight of those unasked questions stayed with me for the next few days.

Leave well enough alone, I kept repeating to myself – and Maria seemed well enough.

We'd always enjoyed a good sex life. I'd reach for her or she'd come to me; body knowing body, her body needing to meld with my body. I represented strength and heat, she cool fragility. Without fail we turned each other on. I would say she empowered me while she liked the feeling that I had the strength to crush her, yet never did.

A few nights later we lay in bed. It was a hot night. We'd left the windows open and the blinds undrawn. Maria lay with her back to me facing the window. She liked to watch the night sky, the stars and the winking lights of planes. I reached out for her as I'd done hundreds of times before, my arm sliding across her naked body to cup her breast.

"No," she said.

"Yes," I said smilingly.

"No," and she threw off my arm, "Please Stephanie, leave me alone."

"Please Maria, I don't want to leave you alone." My hand rested lightly on her hip.

In a cold little voice she said, "Touch me again and I'll sleep in the spare room."

"But what have I done?"

She didn't answer. She drew her legs up to her body. Pulled the duvet around her. All I could see were her dark curls but I could feel how tense she was. Then gradually her body relaxed, the hunched outline of her shoulder became a curve. I heard a low regular sound, like the subdued purr of a cat, at first distinct then fading away. I sat up in bed. Without touching her I leant across. She was in a deep sleep. Nothing feigned.

The next morning I was up and out of the house before she woke. Even then I couldn't help myself. I went into the garden and cut a rose, pale pink. I snipped off the thorns and crushed the stem, put it in a glass of water and left it holding down the corner of a sheet of note paper. "I love you," I wrote.

"... words such as ROMANTIC LOVE are used to stand for a set of ideas, characteristic physiological states and behaviours. A higher emotion is not a pure mental state but something more akin to a script we have internalised and learnt to act out..."

A few days later, because the weather was so good, we took a couple of deckchairs into the garden. Maria talked about the shrubs she intended to plant come autumn, an area of groundsel and ivy she would dig over and turn into a starting bed for cuttings. I'd been enthusiastic in the bumbling way that, in the past, had always made her laugh affectionately.

"So Stephanie, what are those?" she said mischievously, pointing to a clump of blue flowers.

"Haven't a clue. Foxgloves?"

"You do know," she insisted.

"I don't."

"Well you should after all this time. Delphiniums, you idiot."

She leant forward as if to kiss me. Automatically I half closed my eyes and puckered up, pushing my face close to hers. I felt her recoil and she spat – angrily, like a cat spits when under attack. It shocked us both. She sat back in the deckchair and rubbed her mouth with the back of her right hand as if she couldn't believe her own reaction.

Half crying, she said, "I'm sorry. But don't ever do that again."

"Do what? Kiss you? Weren't you about to kiss me?"

She looked bewildered, spoke as if talking to herself, "I don't think I was. I don't think that's something I would do now."

Her words chilled me. I took out my handkerchief and wiped the spit from my cheek. "Why's that?" I asked.

"I don't like it."

"What? I don't believe you."

She shut her eyes. The right eye closed before the left. I was becoming as hypersensitive as she was.

"Believe it," she said. That was it. She refused to say any more.

It remained a beautiful day. I brought out a book. Maria changed into her bikini and lay on a lounger, her eyes hidden behind sunglasses. Several times I realised she was crying. I couldn't comfort her. I didn't dare.

At one point after a long silence I said, "What about seeing a doctor?"

"Not necessary," she said.

"But surely?"

"No."

Without speaking we remained outside till six o'clock.

*

I tried to be clever, to show affection almost in passing. Her responses were varied: more of the spitting, an unnerving "Hah" sound as if she were trying to clear a rush of air from the back of her throat. Or she'd smack me away or cringe as if avoiding a blow. In the end, she dealt with it, because I couldn't. She kept something between us – the table, chairs, even a rucksack worn as I've seen mothers carrying their babies, against her breasts.

"I would never hurt you," I told her.

"You won't get the chance." Her voice with that harsh warning note I was growing used to.

Sometimes she'd shake her head and look puzzled as if for a second she knew she was using someone else's script. "I'm sorry, Stephanie. I am sorry," she'd say. But if I took as much as a step towards her, that damn left lid would fold over her eye: "Don't!"

"I'm cool. Keep calm. When you're ready." And I'd back away.

After that initial visit to Maria's mother, I never saw her again. She died just over a year ago, before Maria changed so completely; but not in hospital. She was sent home because there was nothing more the doctors could do and Maria went back to Fern Lodge to look after her. I missed her terribly. I feared her mother's influence, feared Maria's return to the life they'd shared – Maria sleeping in that white-painted single bed, getting up every morning and padding over to the window. That perfect view out over the sea.

One evening Maria telephoned.

"Mum's dead," she said.

"I'm sorry." Then, too quickly, "When will you be coming home?"

"Soon."

The funeral passed and still Maria didn't come. I tried to put no further pressure on her. I was sympathetic and loving on the telephone. In the end I broke and late one night I begged, "Maria, please come home. I'm lost without you."

I didn't cry but my voice shook. A silence on the line, then she said, "Don't worry. I'll be back on Saturday."

That was a Tuesday. Every day till Saturday I rang Maria but to no response. I thought, if she doesn't turn up on Saturday, I'll damn well drive down and bring her back by force if I have to.

There was no need for force. At dusk she came home. I heard her car. By the time I'd reached the front door and thrown it open, she was already on the path. She was as grey as the light. Like a wraith she passed back into our house.

Gradually I believed we were returning to a loving normality.

Maria has annexed the box room for herself. When I'm at home she stays in there for hours. We've bought her a single bed. She made me leave it at the door.

"I'll manage," she said politely, as if she were a student making herself at home in a stranger's house. I went downstairs, loitering between the kitchen and hallway, listening to boxes being shifted and then the bed being dragged across the floorboards. Now there are unfamiliar single duvet covers and single fitted sheets whirling around on the clothes line.

In the garden, the patch of groundsel and ivy never got dug over. This autumn no cuttings were taken. I tidied up on my own, standing in the half light watching the orange flames shoot up from my bonfire. Lonely.

She still eats dinner with me at the kitchen table, although any gestures like my lighting candles or dimming the light she deals with. Snuffs out the candles between her thumb and first finger, turns up the dimmer switch so that the light shines even brighter than usual. She makes these actions briskly, as if righting a wrong, with no reference to me. Also, she refuses all offers of alcohol. Once when I'd had much too much to drink I poured her out a glass of white wine. I chose it especially; the same Muscadet she'd drunk that day with her mother.

"No, Stephanie."

"Why not?"

"There doesn't have to be a reason."

I tried to force it down her. She put up no fight, but nor was she going to let the rim of the wine glass get between her lips. The glass would have to break first. When I realised that, I stopped. I threw the glass at the wall.

"How did your mother really die?" I snarled at her.

"You know she died of cancer," she said, before relenting. "Right up to the last, she tried to swim each day. She still had bottles and bottles of codeine, all out of date, in her bedroom cupboard. One afternoon she took a bottle of codeine and a bottle of wine down to the sea. The next morning her body was washed up on the beach."

"Did you know what she intended to do?"

"Yes. I carried the bottles."

She's away for weeks at a time now. I've offered to leave. I've asked her if she'd like to leave. We could sell the house and divide up the money. She shakes her head and doesn't answer. She hardly talks at all. Is this a regression or a deliberate withdrawal? She's learning to write with her left hand.

"Did your mother write with her left hand? Did your

grandmother? Who? Was it your elusive father?" Questions do me no good.

While she's away, I sit in her room and sift through boxes and boxes of theories, research, the harebrained and the serious. My own innocent 'areas of unsafety', brought into the house and stored in what should have been a nursery.

Thousands of words calling up something or someone – that is linked to Maria, that was once left-handed. There is something about the sea and something more about Maria becoming the child I felt was waiting for me. Something that can't bear to be touched and can't allow itself to accept my love.

Fit

I don't really understand Pat's popularity, particularly with younger women. Pat's quite old – 'elderly' they'd call her on Radio 4 News. Fifty-two – younger than me, but to be honest you wouldn't think it.

For instance – last Thursday. We'd been invited (along with about a hundred and fifty other women of our ilk) to the launch of a famous lesbian chanteuse's autobiography.

Fancy dress was optional but of course we both dressed up. The two of us (we're not a couple, never were, never will be) are known for our fondness for costume which our other friend, Joan (who's been in and out of therapy for years), says can often signify a dislike of 'self'.

I thought I looked pretty spiffing in a Burton suit, double breasted, wide lapelled, purchased from my local charity shop; shirt and tie also from the same establishment. I'd borrowed my brother's natty brown trilby. I'm still fairly slim and above average height so I can carry off a bit of cross-dressing rather successfully. I'd travelled up to London on the train and sensed that the glances I got from my few fellow passengers were curious but not uncomplimentary.

At Charing Cross I met Pat pacing up and down outside Next, expression dour.

"I'm bloody frozen," were her first words. "I've had two Big

Macs and a mega-sized hot chocolate to warm me up and now I feel bloated and unhealthy."

"Hello Pat. What's happened to your face? Gone three rounds with the girlfriend?"

Pat's hand shot up to what looked like a nasty cut on her cheek. "It's a pimple," she said, "Does it show?"

"I'll say it does..."

"Look, I need to go into Next. I want to check this woolly hat in their mirror."

Into Next we went. Their sale was still on – last few days. The staff, just ready to shut up shop for the night, looked at us askance. Under Pat's trench coat she wore military gear: camouflage combats and tee-shirt, khaki leg-warmers rolled to look like puttees over her leather walking boots (still muddy from her disastrous walking holiday in the Peak District, which I won't go into now). In front of a mirror she tried out various alluring or otherwise ways to wear a brown knitted hat, while I feigned interest in a fuchsia cardigan with ruffled front, to appease the restless sales personnel.

"How do I look?" she asked.

"Fabulous" – which wasn't true but, as Joan says, Pat can't take negative feedback.

The venue near Trafalgar Square was packed. Ratio of drink to food about seventy-thirty, ratio of costumed to uncostumed guests, fifty-fifty. I've noticed during my decades of dressing up that those who don't, tend to take themselves rather more seriously than those who do, with the exception of those who dress up for a living such as, say, Imelda Staunton (not at this gathering, but one of my own personal showbiz favourites).

At the far end of the room was a small stage. Three women dressed as Wrens (they may have been Wrens) were singing the 1965 Keely Smith hit, 'You're Breaking My Heart', which was also the title of the famous lesbian chanteuse's autobiography.

"That brings back memories." I turned to Pat but she'd already commandeered a glass of red wine and, with it held above her head, dour expression changed to one of supreme satisfaction, was heading for the tiny dance floor. You see, Pat was in her element.

In quick succession I drank two glasses of white wine, with a still-water chaser to maintain my equilibrium, then went in search of Joan. Me and Joan, we get on rather well. We put this down to both being Virgoans which Pat says equals 'one pair of fusspots'.

Spotted Joan. I had a piece of information regarding myself to impart. The previous week when I'd been at a celebration for the Chinese New Year, a reliable source had told me that, as an Ox, I was a possible leader of men – or in my case women. I'd asked after Joan and she was a Rabbit, pleasant enough but not a leader of anybody. Pat was a snake. No surprises there.

"I see Pat's enjoying herself," observed Joan before I could begin. Joan wasn't in fancy dress although she'd had the hairdresser carve a pound sign into her cropped hair just above her forehead which I chose not to comment on.

"Is she? I'm so relieved. Book launches aren't really her thing."

"Don't worry about it. She's dancing."

"I wasn't worrying..." Yes, Pat was dancing. With an attractive dark-haired woman in a black velvet trouser suit. "Isn't that the famous chanteuse's agent?"

"Yes. What's Pat done to her face?"

"She says it's a pimple."

"Looks more like she's been in a fight," Joan sniffed. "Some women go for that 'damaged' look."

"Do they? I was going to offer my beige concealer but you know how prickly Pat can be."

Joan said, "To change the subject a tad, a woman patted my bottom just now with more than sisterly pressure."

"What did you do?"

"Nothing. I'm waiting to see what her game is." Joan gulped from her glass of fresh orange juice. She won't touch alcohol. Says she has a nervous reaction to it. Won't even eat wine gums or put a dribble of sherry in her boeuf bourguignon.

"So?" I prompted.

"So nothing. She took her hand away after a few seconds. Still, from little acorns etcetera."

In silence we watched Pat dancing enthusiastically to the Wrens' rendition of 'Chattanooga Choo Choo'.

"Why don't you bring me on home?" Pat sang out, her voice loud and slightly drunk-sounding, above the polite murmur of revellers. I winced. Turned back to Joan to share my news about Ox and Rabbit.

"I'm off to mingle," she said.

"Me too," I said.

What a wonderful evening! Had another glass of wine, several unspecifiable vol au vents and at least a dozen mini sausage rolls. Bought a copy of *You're Breaking My Heart* and got the famous chanteuse to sign it. Was rather disappointed that she didn't once look into my eyes – they are my best feature and ageless. Like Joan I mingled a good deal, exchanging pleasantries, tipping my trilby at personable people. Joan reported back with news of further pats on her bottom which made me wonder if her admirer wasn't in fact a clumsy pickpocket. However, no pickpocketing to report in my own buttock area. Back to famous lesbian chanteuse to apologise for Pat destroying the card table bearing the display of her autobiography.

"Pat is so-oh very clumsy."

"Don't worry about it," she said laughingly.

"Oh, I wasn't worrying *per se*," I said, also laughingly.

Went in search of Pat. Found her still sticking like glue to agent. Both looked cheerful, sipping from the same beaker of red wine. Made another circuit of the room and finally cornered the agent on her own.

"You don't know me..." I began.

"No I don't."

"I'm a friend of Pat. You danced with her earlier."

"I did indeed and hope to do so again."

"I just want to apologise on her behalf, she can be impossible."

"Can she?" Agent raised her beautifully pencilled eyebrows. "I look forward to that. She's very fit, isn't she? I'd better get hold of her before the music packs up."

For some minutes I stood alone feeling I don't know quite what. Like a prize... fusspot? Joined Joan, who was slumped rag-doll fashion against the wall.

"All right, Joan?"

"I've overdosed on fresh orange. You can do that, you know."

"So I've heard. Look here, Pat's new agent friend reckons Pat's 'very fit'. Now what do you think she means? 'Fit' as in attractive or 'fit' as in athletically able?"

"We all know what 'fit' means," Joan responded with unnecessary irritation, "I expect she meant both of those, although I can't for the life of me imagine why."

We watched Pat and the agent foxtrotting. Had to admit

that they danced well together: same height, same build, same rather over-excitable expressions on their faces. Quite an age disparity, Pat being a good fifteen years older.

Joan said gloomily, "They're getting on like a house on fire," and I neighed back, "I'm surprised. I'd have thought that a pimple the size of a sixpence would be a complete turn-off."

"What's a sixpence?"

"Oh really, Joan, don't be obtuse. I'm getting my coat."

We were all getting our coats. The main lights switched on and the singing Wrens marched briskly off their makeshift stage. Pat finally emerged from the scrum heading for the cloakroom, grinning – that horrible expression – from ear to ear.

"Great evening," she said breathlessly.

"I've had my bottom touched at least five times," Joan said. "In fact I wouldn't be surprised to find some discolouration of the skin by morning."

"How about you?" Pat turned to me. "Anyone been touching your bum?"

"I've experienced the enveloping warmth of loving friendship all night."

"That's a 'no' then?"

Pat's popularity continued into the queue for our coats. Several times she was kissed by complete strangers. I definitely saw admiring glances lingering on what was in truth a pimple. Pat's agent friend held on to her hand for ages.

"Such an amazing grip," she enthused, "I really like you. Has anyone ever told you, you have a fabulous face?"

Joan and I exchanged bewildered glances and refrained from snorting. I whispered, "She's young enough to be Pat's daughter."

"Granddaughter."

Pat's 'fabulous face' was 'wreathed' in smiles – a rare sight since she'd reached fifty.

"Why not come along to the pub with me?" the agent enticed.

Pat hesitated.

"Don't mind us," Joan said with a stiff little laugh. I buttoned up my overcoat and straightened my trilby, cramming it further down on my head lest a gust of wind whipped it away once we got outside.

"Thanks but no," Pat said, "I'm with my friends."

Joan and I waited while she retrieved her trench coat, kissed a few more women, squeezed a few more hands. Finally the three of us set off into the freezing night.

"Only ten o'clock," I said. "There's time for a pizza before I catch my train."

"My buttocks are smarting," Joan said, but good naturedly. "I hope they've got comfy banquettes."

Pat said nothing. She lit a cigarette and strolled along peaceably between us.

"You really shouldn't smoke," I said.

"You're quite right," Pat said and blew a perfect circle into the cold night air.

Hotel du Lac

Silvia's mother once asked Silvia why she always referred to the people in her office as 'colleagues'.

"Surely they must have names? 'Colleague' is such an impersonal word, darling. Aren't colleagues what doctors have, as in, I'll get my colleague to take a look at your X-ray?"

"Mother, these are not people I'd choose to rub shoulders with, that's all. I like to maintain a distance."

Silvia's mother had snorted deliciously and said, "But darling, if you don't watch your step you'll be left on the shelf."

"I'm only twenty-two."

"You won't be 'only twenty-two' forever. You have a nice flat, earn a good salary; all you need is some good-looking fella to share it with. Remember, *Who is Silvia? What is she that all our swains commend her?*"

"I don't need the commendation of any swains, thank you."

Twenty years sped by. For the fourth time Silvia's mother was seriously considering remarriage or at least a romantic sojourn in Hawaii, while Silvia, still unattached, had booked a fortnight's holiday at the Hotel du Lac on the Norfolk coast.

The brochure had shown a picture of a white-haired couple toasting each other against a backdrop of French windows opening onto a sparkling blue sea. The sea looked almost Mediterranean. Although Silvia hadn't been to the Mediterranean, she had seen brochures: colleagues at work poring over pictures of Ithaca, Paxos and Benidorm.

"I don't suppose there is a lake?" she'd queried on the telephone.

"There's a toddlers' pool and a sun lounge." The receptionist's tone had been truculent.

"I'd like a table with a sea view in the dining room, preferably near the French windows."

"We don't have French windows."

"In the brochure you do."

There was no immediate reply, only the crackling sound of a sweet being unwrapped, then a final, "I'll see what I can arrange," spoken slowly as if through a mouthful of toffee.

Later, in her kitchen, making a cup of Earl Grey tea, she considered the words 'sea view' and how deceitfully seductive they could sound. How a holiday by the sea must always be a failure if the sea couldn't be viewed from some point within the holiday accommodation.

Privately (so private she hardly dared acknowledge them to herself), Silvia cherished hopes about this holiday, that she, like the dowdy Edith in Anita Brookner's novel, *Hotel du Lac*, would be singled out by a supremely attractive, world-weary 'someone'.

Silvia's *Rough Guide to England* described the hotel as 'flamboyantly gothic'. Her initial impression, approaching it through a dense sea mist, was that 'eerily gothic' would have been more appropriate. On entering the vast marble atrium, several dusty chandeliers shedding a sickly yellow light onto a huge expanse of medallioned carpet, she changed again to 'drearily not gothic'.

"I'm Ms Parsons," she said, louder than she'd intended, to the woman bent over a ledger in the reception alcove. The woman raised her head; a dour yet strong face, dark hair flecked with silver, unfriendly grey eyes. The woman was chewing. *Ah yes, the toffee masticator,* Silvia thought, and for some reason she found herself blushing.

"Mrs Parsons?"

"No, Ms Parsons."

"Ms Parsons?" The receptionist raised a querying eyebrow and handed Silvia her key. "Third floor. Lift not working. I'm here on my own so you'll have to carry up your suitcase. Ok?"

That evening at dinner, Silvia saw the receptionist again. Their eyes met across a crowded dining room. The receptionist was no longer a receptionist. She wore a white shirt, dark trousers and a small green apron, with a notepad on a piece of string dangling from her trouser pocket. She was now a waitress. Silvia's waitress. Silvia's spirits dropped.

The waitress seemed to work all day and every day. She worked both the breakfast and dinner shift. Silvia thought of her as a grim, reluctant, ill-natured, hostile breed of dog – handsomer than a Rottweiler, possibly a grim, reluctant, ill-natured, hostile elk hound. Further adjectives occurred but she limited herself to just four, aware that this desire to elaborate ad infinitum on difficult situations was becoming an entrenched part of her interior life.

Morning and evening on Silvia's entrance into the dining room, the waitress (Silvia didn't like to ask her name) would sullenly peel herself from the wall behind the condiment trolley and track Silvia to her table, leaving her hardly enough room to pull out her chair and sit down.

Morning:

"Ok, juice or cornflakes?" as Silvia unfolded her paper serviette and spread it on her knees.

"I think juice, please."

"Orange or grapefruit?"

"Grapefruit and then I'll have –"

"I'll take the rest of your order when I bring the juice," said in a surly voice, no hint of a smile.

Evening:

"Pâté or soup of the day?"

"Which is?"

"Wild mushroom."

"Pâté and then I'll have –"

"I'll take the rest of your order when I bring the pâté."

It was a small disagreement, yet the principle irked Silvia. There stood ungracious waitress with notebook and pencil, here sat paying guest. Waitress – paying guest. Surely, Silvia reasoned, it was the paying guest who had every right to say what she wanted and when she wanted to say it? And as invariably she ordered pâté and grapefruit juice, why could she not go straight to her main order?

At one time Silvia had thought very little about what she ate. She'd eaten automatically, her mind dwelling in a romantic daydream where she loved and was loved. A dream of someone strong and caring but taciturn, who would bring about within her a soft flowering. It was possible. And then it seemed to become impossible and, imperceptibly, instead she gave her heart away to food. She thought about it incessantly. After only a few brief hours apart, she looked forward to seeing it again – and surprisingly, although the hotel was dismal, the food was not.

Invariably, the evening meal was delicious. Particularly the pâté, although animal of origin was unclear. And then there was pork, or leg of lamb, turkey, cod on Friday to look forward to; three vegetables, boiled and roast potatoes with thick rich gravy and relevant sauce. Puddings. Her mouth watered at the thought of a steaming treacle pudding sitting stolidly in a sea of creamy yellow custard. Profiteroles! Sometimes she thought that if it came down to a choice between saving her mother from an unspeakable peril or the offer of a large plate of profiteroles (with extra cream)... well there was no contest, her mother would have to just hang on or make other arrangements.

It was Thursday before Silvia woke to a sunny morning. She dressed with care for a day on the beach. Under a pair of raspberry-coloured shorts and white sleeveless ribbed top, she wore her swimsuit. She decided against her usual severe French pleat, leaving her straight brown hair to fall loosely to her shoulders. She added a silver bangle, flared her nostrils, stroked her neck. *You don't look a day over thirty-five,* she told herself before swinging down to breakfast.

In the dining room she rushed across to her table, leaving the waitress sprinting some yards behind. Foregoing the ritual unfolding of the serviette she sang out, "Grapefruit and then I'd like black pudding with –" before her waitress cut her short by almost shouting, "I'll take the rest of your order when I bring the juice."

Five minutes later, as her juice was placed in front of her and the waitress took up her notepad and pencil, Silvia said, "Might I ask –?"

"Black pudding, you said," and the waitress wrote down, 'black pudding'.

"No."

"You don't want black pudding?" The waitress scratched out 'black pudding'.

"Yes, I do want black pudding." The waitress sighed heavily and began to write.

Hurriedly, Silvia said, "I want to know when this tablecloth will be changed. It's filthy."

For a moment the waitress appeared speechless, then she said, "Clean on last Saturday."

"But this is now Thursday."

"Then it will be clean on in two days' time."

"Are you saying, tablecloths are changed only once a week?"

The waitress tapped her teeth with the end of the pencil and scrutinised her notepad. "I'm not saying anything hard and fast – if they're soiled we change or turn them."

"This is soiled." For the first time their eyes engaged. More thoughtful teeth-tapping from waitress.

"Well?" Silvia prompted, suddenly sure that the waitress was trying not to laugh. At a neighbouring table a loving elderly couple paused in toast-buttering to eavesdrop. Silvia felt a tide of red sweep up from beneath the neck of her sleeveless top.

"I'll have it seen to," the waitress said.

"Thank you. So it's black pudding and full English, please?"

The waitress said nothing. Said nothing when she delivered Silvia's breakfast to the table. Silvia had hoped that the waitress might just say something. Not necessarily, *Bon appetit, do make free with the condiment trolley.* But something.

As she ate, Silvia found herself thinking about the waitress. Of her cold grey eyes that mirrored the North Sea (just visible from Silvia's table were she to stand on her chair and crane her neck in an easterly direction). She wondered how it was that the other hotel guests seemed to like her. And why did the waitress seem to like them and not her? Why was she never the recipient of one of the waitress's warm, approving smiles? *After all,* she thought, *I'm unfailingly polite. I open doors for older people, I can talk intelligently on politics or weather, have an extensive knowledge of ornithology and wild flowers. I like music and know a fair bit about Italian wines.* As Silvia listed her many accomplishments, the waitress slipped from her mind. She concluded that she, Silvia, was a rather special person who for too long had been hiding her light under a bushel. *What exactly was a bushel?* Should she join a club? Should she advertise in her local paper when she got home?

GSOH. NS. Nature-loving woman and seasoned traveller in the British Isles, seeks similar.

Changed this to: *Attractive, slim build, lady, GSOH, NS, seeks politically aware, nature-loving gourmet with nostalgic fondness for the great British pudding.*

Changed this to: *Vivacious, intelligent female with quirky taste in travelling, eating and nature seeks a like-minded... woman.*

But what would her mother say? What would the editor of the local paper say? It was a very small local paper. The ads only covered two columns and even then the editor sometimes had to repeat them several times to fill up space. Silvia's mother always read the ads. Silvia could imagine popping over as she always did at Sunday teatime; her mother passing her the newspaper folded at the relevant page. "Guess what, darling, lesbians are advertising in the local. Can you believe it? The same box number's put herself in three times. Better watch your step. You're just the sort lesbians are after: single woman with own property."

"But mother, it's me. I am that advertising lesbian."

Silvia's mother's face crumpling. Silvia's mother looking utterly betrayed.

*

That evening the tablecloth had been turned over so that any stains had become faint discolourations. Some acknowledgement seemed called for: *Ah now that is an improvement. So much better to view stains through a tablecloth darkly, don't you think?* Silvia was not entirely confident she could imbue such a remark with the required careless gaiety and perhaps it would be better suited to literary salons of the Bloomsbury era. So the moment of saying anything passed. Silvia ordered her pâté, accepted it meekly before ordering breast of turkey and chestnut stuffing, accepted it meekly before ordering lemon meringue pie topped with a curlicue of double cream and came at last to the cheese and biscuit end of each evening meal. The waitress produced a side plate displaying a fan of three cream crackers and several squares of vari-coloured cheeses sweating in their plastic sachets. Not to everyone's taste but Silvia, replete, enjoyed lingering over these colourful morsels. Five or six grapes would not have gone amiss but otherwise it was perfectly acceptable with her decaffeinated coffee.

"Not quite finished," Silvia said as the waitress arrived back bearing an empty tray. Silvia hung on to the cheese plate, her own plate, coffee cup and saucer plus an oblong of unopened butter. With a rolled lawn napkin hitherto unseen in the dining room, the waitress began to flick at the sprinkling of cracker and breadcrumbs on the tablecloth.

"I won't be much longer," Silvia said.

As the waitress turned away, Silvia distinctly heard her mutter, "Christ, you don't half make a mess."

"I beg your pardon," spluttered Silvia, but the waitress kept on walking, banging through the swing doors and out into the kitchen.

Silvia inspected the tablecloth. Yes, she had made quite a

mess. Now there was very little difference between either side of the turned cloth; crumbs around her plate, a smear of butter, a spattering of gravy. Was it her fault that the gravy boat poured imperfectly? And did she not have rights? Which brought her back to the paying guest's prerogatives. Surely if she chose to douse the tablecloth in gravy, that was up to her?

However, after further thought she agreed with herself that she didn't want to be seen as a messy eater. Worrying to have been considered annoyingly fastidious for a lifetime, only to find fastidiousness deserting her in her middle years when to be fastidious became an absolute imperative if she didn't want to end up confined like Granny Parsons to a nursing home, dressed in plastic sheeting. From tomorrow onwards she'd pay more attention.

Silvia decided on a walk before retiring. Outside, the setting sun was infusing the sea front with a rosy light. Inside, the gloomy bar interior danced with a myriad grey dust motes. Several people drowsed in armchairs. The television was on but the sound had been turned down in consideration of the sleepers.

An elderly man with greased-back white hair swivelled round on his bar stool to face her. "Fancy a drink?" he said, raising a half-full tumbler.

"No thank you. I'm just off for a stroll. The evening light down here is marvellous," she replied in a voice that reminded her of the comedienne Joyce Grenfell at her most sadly spinsterish.

"Perhaps later." He winked at her.

She walked as far as the pier, a matter of two hundred and fifty yards, and found a bench facing the sun, now dipping down below the horizon. The sky was almost green, streaked with gold and iridescent pink. The evening remained warm, its heat at last having the strange and subtle effect she looked for every year, that made her think of plants crouching in the dark until they couldn't help but respond to the gentle warmth above their heads.

The strings of fairy lights switched on, coloured bulbs watery against the fading day. She felt so at ease, so perfectly happy at that moment, that the thought that she was greedy and no amount of delicious food could satisfy her for long slipped unhindered into her consciousness. Her happiness was transformed to a strange sorrow and self-knowledge. Only when replete could she relax, could she completely give herself up to... well, what the world had to offer. Which was why, in years, she'd never given herself up. In the pocket of her fleece she found a crumpled pink paper serviette and dabbed daintily at her nose.

"Are you ok?"

Silvia recognised the brusque voice of her waitress.

"Fine. Perfect."

The waitress nodded and smirked and slouched away.

Later, Silvia rang her mother from the pay phone in the hotel lobby.

"It's me, Silvia."

"Hello darling. Are you having a fabulous time?"

"Not really. Are you?"

There was a silence.

"Mother?"

"Not as fabulous as usual, darling."

"What's happened?"

"The new man's playing up."

"In what way?"

"Oh, you know – fast and loose." Silvia's mother laughed shakily. "I must be losing my feminine allure."

"Well, perhaps he's not quite right for you. I think you used to set your sights higher."

Silvia heard her mother's sharp intake of breath. "That's a very cruel thing to say. Beggars can't be choosers, as you well know."

"I'm not a beggar. I simply don't choose."

"Nor get chosen."

"I set my sights very high indeed."

"As far as I can see, way up in the wide blue yonder. Let me tell you that any bird in the hand –"

"Please, Mother, I didn't telephone to have an argument."

"Then why did you phone?"

"To hear a familiar voice."

"We are a sad pair." Silvia's mother's voice still crackled with irritation.

"I'm sure you'll sort this new man out or meet someone else. You always do," Silvia said soothingly.

"I do indeed," Silvia's mother said with false gaiety. Silvia could imagine the fine lines on her mother's tired face curving upwards as she smiled and forced sparkle back into her eyes. How exhausting it must be for her, to remain always vivacious. "You get off and enjoy yourself. I'm going to treat myself to a lanolin and rosemary body scrub. Night-night, darling."

"Night-night."

Impossible to change from eating almost anything on offer to a circumspect, *Better not, all things in moderation,* accompanied by a brave smile. On Saturday, Silvia woke early, feeling horribly hungry and depressed. Once again the sun shone. On the Juliet balcony outside her window, a bird that wasn't a seagull was singing. For once Silvia did not reach for her Collins pocket edition of *Birds of the British Isles*.

She dragged herself from her bed and opened the curtains. A glossy male blackbird gave her a beady once-over and seemed to find her gingham pyjamas amusing.

She rapped sharply on the pane. "Clear off." The bird flapped away towards the pier.

"It seems to be a bikini day," Silvia said miserably.

Over her bikini she wore a turquoise shirt that had the option of being buttoned or knotted beneath her breasts. For the first time ever, Silvia chose to knot the shirt. She inspected the revealed area of rib and stomach in the wardrobe mirror and toyed with adding another shirt to hang carelessly over the exposed flesh. She became very angry with her reflection and shouted, "Do I care? Do I really care?" before grabbing up her beach bag and flouncing from her bedroom.

"Juice or cornflakes?" the waitress asked.

"Whatever."

"Juice or cornflakes?"

"Both."

The waitress's eyes snapped from narrowed and disinterested to widely alert. "Not allowed."

"Very well, grapefruit juice."

"You don't have to have grapefruit juice."

"You mean I should have cornflakes?"

"No, you could have orange juice."

"Correction, there's the orange-coloured juice and the grapefruit-coloured juice. None of it's real juice, is it? It's only tincture of a juice. Some diluted muck from the supermarket. Am I right?"

The waitress looked uneasy. "I couldn't say where it came from. Possibly the Unigate milkman, could be Tesco's. I'll bring the grapefruit juice, then?"

"Please do."

From behind morning papers, neighbouring breakfasters

sneaked sly looks at Silvia. *That mousy filly packs quite a nasty temper.* Silvia grinned into the unfolding of her paper serviette. Almost a conversation achieved. Almost a lovers' tiff.

The waitress brought her juice and she ordered a full English breakfast but with only one egg, no sausage or black pudding, making a mental note to treat the clean tablecloth with the utmost care. Silvia finished her juice, finished her half-full English, before moving on to toast and marmalade. She poured out another cup of tea and decided to linger over it, even thought the dining room was emptying.

I am paying for this pleasure. I can sit here for as long or as little as I like. Stoically, Silvia buttered a final slice of toast. Then she eased back her chair, sending a flurry of crumbs onto the floral carpet. Carrying her cup and saucer and slice of toast, her beach bag over one shoulder, she walked out of the dining room. She half expected a cry of, "Oy, just where do you think you're off to with that? Food not allowed outside the dining room." She was aware of her waitress snapping away from the wall. From the remaining tables came a rustle like a breeze through fallen leaves as people gathered up cardigans, handbags, umbrellas and walking sticks. Silvia had initiated an exodus.

Until she'd crossed the road in front of the hotel to the sea wall, she didn't pause. She hoiked herself up onto the wall and struck a casual and suitable pose for sea-wall sitting. Slowly she ate her toast, reflecting on how her spirits could so easily dip and rise. Her head was now a vessel of sun-filled light. Nearby, a black-headed gull loitered. Should she become a twitcher? Was is it only her imagination or did she have a genuine rapport with nature, particularly of the wingèd kind? Would that follow with bats and butterflies (hopefully charming wingèd kinds)? She wouldn't like to submit to the fond attentions of say, a swarm of locusts. Suddenly life felt good. No, life need not be all about food.

The gull muttered something agreeable and looked seawards. Silvia looked seawards. She thought of her mother. Between them stood a snow-capped mountain. On the far side, Silvia's mother, buffeted by wind and the weight of shifting snow, was heading reluctantly downwards. And there was Silvia, pretty close to the summit, having toiled through some seriously unspectacular terrain. A lesson to be learnt, Silvia thought. No point reaching the summit if the view was to remain uninspiring; she must lift up her head, toss back her hair, stick out nose, chin, breasts.

Between Silvia's squaring shoulder blades she felt an itch, plus a light but intrusive prickle at the base of her scalp. She gave in to an overwhelming desire to look back at the hotel. Nothing much of interest. Although the sky was blue and the temperature climbing, a man and a woman were easing themselves into fur-lined raincoats. Two floors above, her own bedroom window was open and the maid leant on the rail of the balcony smoking a cigarette. If Silvia wasn't mistaken she was also reading her holiday copy of *Hotel du Lac*. Oh, and the waitress. There she was, framed in the faux French windows, looking directly, not at the sea, but at Silvia. She saw that the waitress stood alone with only her tray for company. That the waitress was smiling at her in a way Silvia had noticed men had often smiled at her mother, years ago, at the beginning of a relationship, as if her mother were a dear and lovable creature. The waitress raised the tray to ear level in mock salute. Tentatively, Silvia smiled back.

Shush

"One for the ladies, I think," Martin says without glancing up from his bulky paperback, *How to Make a Billion Pounds without Leaving the Comfort of Your Armchair*.

"Oh, come with us, darling. People will think Margaret and I are an item," Deirdre says, pinching his cheek.

"No, they won't." Martin's cheek veers away from Deirdre's fingers.

"Why do you have such lubbly jubbly cheeks if you won't let me pinch them?"

"I've no idea," Martin replies dryly. He grabs his book and takes the stairs two at a time, heading for the privacy of their bathroom.

Deirdre says Martin spends most of the day in the bathroom. She's considered setting up an office for him in what is now the airing cupboard. He eats and reads sitting on the toilet, she tells me. It's true, on the one occasion I've used their bathroom, I noted a plate with cake crumbs on a stack of books next to the lavatory.

While Deirdre goes upstairs to disentangle her blonde curls and choose between a black feather boa, which suits her, or Martin's twenty-year-old college scarf, which doesn't, I make myself comfortable on their white leather settee. I find myself thinking about my mother, who died a year ago this month, how she used to tell friends that Robert Mitchum could park his shoes under her bed any night of the week. This an impossibility, as Mum's bed was divan-style, leaving only an inch between it and the carpet – about enough room for Robert Mitchum's spectacles. ('Parking his shoes' statement made after seeing RM in second *Cape Fear* with Robert De Niro, when RM was quite elderly.)

"Oh please," interrupts Deirdre (she's opted for the boa), "You've got that rotten reminiscing-about-dead-mother look on your face. Why can't you live in the here and now? How do I look?"

"Fabulous" – if somewhat over-dressed. Black boa, silk trouser suit over magenta silk blouse. She leans on the banister and shouts up, "Martin, it's your last chance to change your mind."

"Fuck off," he calls down good-naturedly.

"I love it when he talks dirty, but I wish he'd shut the door when he's on the toilet."

Exit the two of us, laughing.

I queue for the tickets. The film is *Pride and Prejudice*. The foyer's packed with women, a few men looking slightly adrift. There goes inimitable Deirdre battling through the mêlée to get to the ice creams. She flings open the door of the freezer and bawls across the crowd, "I'm having Bailey's. What flavour do you want?"

"Black Forest Gateau," I bawl back.

From the freezer, she heads for the counter. She is a sizable woman wearing a mean, no-nonsense expression on her face – the group of sensibly dressed middle-aged women fall back and let her push in front of them. She buys a large carton of toffee-flavoured popcorn plus an economy size bag of M&M's.

Going up the staircase to Cinema 1, I say, "I'm not fond of M&M's, Deirdre."

"Good. More for me."

There's a cheeky, childlike quality to Deirdre's absolute commitment to putting herself first that amuses me. We choose our usual seats. When Martin is with us, he sits next to the aisle, then me in the middle, then Deirdre.

"Bloody good job Martin didn't come with us – all these women would have given him the heebie-jeebies," Deirdre says through a mouth stuffed with popcorn.

Martin only likes people if they're in a club or a pub, but not at his table or standing too close to him at the bar. He doesn't much like men, because they make him feel competitive; he doesn't much like women because they make him feel awkward. He quite likes me because I'm a lesbian, a non-threatening hybrid.

A nudge from Deirdre. "On your marks," she says.

As always, we roar with laughter at the Orange advert, although we agree they're not as funny as they used to be. The best Orange adverts were when a romance seemed to be developing between the slimy, go-getting boss and his plain, equally slimy number two. Deirdre drags her feather boa under her nose and says she doesn't remember anything like that happening. Deirdre always insists she loves 'gay people', she just doesn't want them in her face. Deirdre also agrees with my dead mum that the word 'gay' used to be such a jolly, useful word, but unlike my mum she doesn't intend to use it all the time to make a point – although old people can get away with that sort of thing, young people (Deirdre) would be considered weird.

"Get stuck in," Deirdre says re my ice-cream tub. She's finished hers. "Oh-oh, we're off."

She upends her tub over her face to catch the last drop of Bailey's. A rustle of excitement runs through the packed cinema, sweet wrappers are extinguished, conversations fade – here is Elizabeth Bennet played by Keira Knightley, here is Elizabeth Bennet's ramshackle family. Time passes. I am engrossed in the film, apart from an awareness of Deirdre's plump hand plying its way between the M&M's packet and her mouth. Very slowly, she leans towards me and whispers, "She's got no bosoms."

"But she's very pretty," I whisper back.

"Do you think so? She reminds me of Winona Ryder and we all know what happened to her."

"Do we?"

A woman in the row behind hisses, "Shush."

"Shush yourself," Deirdre says, but she subsides back on to her side of the arm rest. Then, "The penny's just dropped. The dad's Donald Sutherland. Hasn't he aged? Apart from his teeth."

I nod briskly and rearrange myself in the seat to discourage any further outburst from Deirdre.

"Do you think they're false?"

Ignore her. Privately agree that his teeth do look extraordinary. Disturbing. The kind of teeth you'd expect the Big Bad Wolf to have rather than fatherly Mr Bennet.

Deirdre says, "What was that film where he was stabbed to death by the dwarf in the red sou'wester?"

"Will you be quiet?" the woman behind us says quite loudly. She lays a hand on Deirdre's silken shoulder, which is unwise.

"Oy, oy, oy," Deirdre says, "Who you molesting?"

Woman smartly removes her hand, "I'm merely asking you to keep quiet."

"Merely asking..." Deirdre mimics a posh voice completely

unlike the woman's. "Actually it was more like telling, not asking at all."

From all sides of the audience we are now being shushed.

"That's enough, Deirdre," I snap. "Sorry," I say to the woman, who smiles stiffly.

Again Deirdre subsides. Mouths 'traitor' at me.

I try to concentrate on the film. Miss Bennet is dancing with Mr Darcy who possesses a thunderous brow. However, there is a definite frisson of attraction between them which is as it should be. Which prompts me to think of my all-time favourite cinematic coupling (romantic rather than carnal), Fred Astaire and Ginger Rogers... But I'm not allowed to think about them for long – Elizabeth Bennet is taunting Mr Darcy, who is looking even more troubled and thunderous. In fact, I could almost start laughing. Realise that yes, Deirdre actually is laughing – more a disparaging chortle.

This film is not for her. Nobody has been shot and she knows that nobody will be shot. There is nothing to look forward to, and she is a woman who likes to look forward. She bangs down the empty seat next to her and wedges her popcorn carton into an upright position so she can better rummage in her bag of M&M's. Bag suddenly splits and M&M's cascade onto the floor.

"Sod it," she says and starts scrabbling after them.

I grab her arm. "Deirdre, no. It's filthy down there. You can't possibly eat sweets that have rolled on the floor."

"Try me." Her voice is muffled by hair, boa and by her head plunging between her knees. I take hold of her shoulders and pull her back up. She blows out her cherub lips like a naughty, restless pony.

"Here, finish my tub," I offer.

She takes it.

"You're a slow-coach," she says. "Ok, what's happening?"

"Romantic misunderstandings."

"Tell me about them."

"I just did."

I like the way Deirdre eats my ice cream with her mouth open like a child. And with disbelief on her face like a canny child.

"I can't get on with Keira," she whispers.

Find myself also dissatisfied with Keira Knightley – her ability to make her eyes fill with tears at every small setback. I'm also distracted by her eyeliner and the whites of her eyes being a little pink. Feel that my own heroine, Nicole Kidman... but stop myself from going any further because Nicole is too old to play Elizabeth Bennet. Nicole is a woman and Keira is still a girl. Is that why I'm disenchanted? Because I like women now, not girls?

"Would he really fall in love with a woman with no bosoms?"

I whisper back, "Bosoms aren't everything."

"Get real. All men like bosoms, present company excluded."

"I'm not a man."

"You know what I mean."

"Actually, I don't. Sometimes, Deirdre, you can be very ignorant," I snap back.

"Ignorant. Moi?"

Behind us, the woman who'd complained jumps up, grabs her coat and bag, and rushes up the aisle to the exit.

"What's her problem?" Deirdre says. "Now correct me if I'm wrong, but would any bloke go charging round the countryside in his dressing gown on behalf of Keira Knightley?"

"Martin might like her."

"Martin? My Martin? Would he have settled for these," she

thumps her ample breasts, "if he'd wanted a stick-thin young girl?"

No time to reply, as a man in a cheap maroon dinner jacket, accompanied by complaining woman, is shining a torch on us and saying urgently, "Come on. Out of it," as if he's discovered a couple of kids ripping up the seats.

"The film's not finished yet, mate," Deirdre says.

"I'm the manager, not your mate, and it has as far as you're concerned."

"Me and my partner visit this cinema at least twice a week..."

"Well, you and your partner are barred from now on."

The woman says, "Actually, her partner wasn't the one making all the noise."

I smirk gratefully, which I know isn't admirable. Deirdre shoots to her feet, sending a jet of M&M's and popcorn over the row in front. "Eeugh, she's not my partner," she squeals, "I'm not a bloody lezzer."

"Deirdre," I... expostulate.

From several rows back, someone lobs an empty ice-cream tub at her. She neatly bats it away and it flies past the manager's ear.

"You bloody fuckers," Deirdre shouts at everyone.

"You bloody lezzer," someone shouts back.

Deirdre, hands on hips, hair and boa in fabulous disarray, rounds on the disembodied voice while behind her Mr Darcy embraces Elizabeth Bennet. "Do I look like a lesbian?" Deirdre demands.

"Yes!" The entire audience is in agreement.

"You bastards."

Deirdre pushes past me, past the manager, who raises his torch as if fending off a blow, past the complainant, who is using the manager's body as a shield, and storms up the aisle accompanied by loud cheering and stamping of feet. Sheepishly, I follow her out. No cheer for me. A couple of boos, which I consider unfair.

We adjourn to the Tempo Coffee Lounge in the precinct. Am considering whether to take Deirdre to task re her anti-lesbian sentiments; however, she seems so cheerful, so energised, that I think, "What is the point?"

"Wasn't that a laugh?" she says, rubbing her hands gleefully. "Be honest. The film was utter crap. They should have got someone like Tom Hanks for Darcy. He'd have lightened things up. Now, who would you choose for Elizabeth Bennet? And don't say Nicole Kidman or Sharon Stone. Think while I ring Martin."

I attempt to think but am distracted by two other Coffee Lounge customers at a table by the window. Man in anorak with a perfectly tempting fudge brownie on a plate in front of him, choosing to lick his female companion's ear. Force my attention back to Deirdre.

"We're in Tempo," she tells Martin, "Been chucked out of the cinema... Having tea and cake... See ya in five." Turns to me. "Look, I'm sorry about the lezzer stuff. I'd love to be a lezzer. Living with a man is no bed of roses. There – I've said I'm sorry and I always say I'll never say I'm sorry. Love is never having to say, etcetera. Keep thinking. Carrot cake or coffee gateau?"

Have still not come up with a suggestion for Elizabeth Bennet and Mr Darcy by the time Martin arrives. Toy with Fred and Ginger but Deirdre and Martin will pooh-pooh that. Agree (with whom?) it is a mad idea but it could have worked. Once Martin is comfortably settled behind his cappuccino and slab of Dundee cake, Deirdre asks which names might have persuaded him to see the film with us.

Quick as a flash he says, "Woody Harrelson and Juliette Lewis."

"Brilliant," Deirdre says.

"But weren't they in *Natural Born Killers*? I don't remember much 'romance'."

"There was romance by the bucket," Deirdre says, "They were soul mates. How many times have we watched that film on DVD, Martin?"

"Dozens."

"We're just like Woody and Juliette, aren't we, darling?" She lunges across the table to pinch his cheek.

"Get off," he says, and knocks her hand away.

Love Me or Leave Me

Yesterday my brother telephoned with the news that Malcolm Chapman had committed suicide. Nothing spectacular, but the coroner's report made the local paper. *Death of much loved doctor,* ran the headline. The newspaper said he'd taken an overdose of sleeping tablets together with a half bottle of whisky. My brother was surprised that I wasn't as shocked as he'd expected. My calm, quiet response disappointed him.

"Well Maggie, you always were a cold fish," he said – which isn't entirely true.

"Steven, I knew already," I said.

My first impulse on putting down the receiver was to ring Avril. Instead, I went out into my new, autumnal garden and began to clear the fallen leaves.

In early middle age I'd finally broken away from the small Hertfordshire town where I'd lived since childhood and moved to Hastings on the south coast. The town was different enough for me to feel my life had made some progress at last, yet so comfortingly similar that I felt unthreatened by that progress.

Recently I read an article about gardens needing to be places of excitement where your heart rate speeds up a beat or two as you step outside. I wonder what Malcolm would have made of that? His garden was a pleasure to work in. It was *his* garden, nothing at all to do with his wife, Avril. She said as long as she had a patch of lawn to put her deckchair on and not too much overhanging foliage blocking out the sunlight, she couldn't care less what went on anywhere else.

They'd lived in the same house for ten years. For the last three I was their gardener – until I moved down here. I didn't like all of my clients but I liked the Chapmans. I liked the companionship of Avril's regular mugs of tea and that the surgery's French windows were always left open, even when the weather was blustery. I asked Malcolm once if his patients minded so very much fresh air. He'd smiled and said, "I have had some grumbles but when I explain that the view over the garden is restorative for both me and them, they tend to back down. And of course there is the electric bar fire." He'd laughed then: "Probably two out of the three colds I treat each week are caught in my surgery."

Restorative – that was a word Malcolm used a lot. I like it. A soothing word.

The Chapmans were of similar height and colouring. Both had dark brown hair with very little grey. He was a few inches taller but they shared the same spare build and unlined faces. Avril's face was strong rather than pretty, but from a distance I could see the striking young couple they must have once made. Only close to, the impression adjusted itself and I saw that no magic dust had saved them from the same fate of aging that the majority of us share.

Personally, I've never been beautiful or even pretty; or if at some moment in my life I ever was, I wasn't aware of it. Malcolm had possessed, in Avril's words, an uncommon masculine beauty. She'd talked to me about this 'beauty' of his as if it had once been a great friend of theirs whom they no longer saw. Not that

Malcolm, in his mid-fifties, had aged badly – on the contrary, he was still a handsome man. A handsome, middle-aged man.

I envied them a little. Their life seemed to be one of peace and content. They appeared to have no worries. However, during my months working in their garden I added to this observation – they seemed to have no family, apart from a son living in Canada, and no friends either. There were Malcolm's patients, his receptionist, Mrs Dilmann the cleaning woman and me. The Chapmans rarely went out in the evenings, not even to a restaurant. A few times Malcolm went away for a conference, but in all the time I worked for them, he never stayed away overnight. Their life was spent within the boundaries of their home.

Once, Avril said, as if in reply to a question I might have thought but hadn't asked, "We like to keep ourselves to ourselves. Right from the beginning we've always been enough company for one another."

If they'd imagined for a moment that one day I'd be sitting companionably in the back of their car or wedged between them in the local cinema, they'd have run a mile. Without intending to, they warmed to my stolid presence in their garden.

Malcolm had to talk to me about what he wanted. Gardening was his passion and he hated not having sufficient time to devote to it any more. In my first few weeks he treated me as if I was his enemy, a stranger brought in to usurp what was his alone. My 'cold fish' approach stood me in good stead. As Malcolm's garden was restorative, so my cool presence reassured. He gained confidence in my work and in me as a person. All my suggestions were tentative. My manner – that old-fashioned word, amiable. With Avril I was the same. A little more relaxed, because it's hard to maintain much reserve with someone bringing out mugs of tea and a biscuit barrel in the shape of Humpty Dumpty three times a day. And it was hard for her to maintain reserve with another woman willing to discuss the merits of chocolate chip cookies versus a plain and wholesome digestive.

I don't fool myself that I became irreplaceable to the Chapmans. What I believe my presence did was to release some of the unacknowledged tension building up between them. I arrived in their lives just as Malcolm began to be aware of a dissatisfaction, like the first niggling harbinger of illness.

It wasn't that Malcolm didn't love his wife. I very clearly saw that he did. But his love for her was no longer of primary interest. Not passionate. Not novel. Not even 'restorative' any more.

I'm concerned that my story is setting up the expectation of a love affair when all I'm trying to do is fathom the reasons behind Malcolm's suicide. The mind, my mind, isn't easy to organise; thoughts are like chickens strutting off in all directions. Here is the good Doctor Chapman... off goes Exact Knowledge heading for the shrubbery and there is Surmise turning over a few seeds in the dirt.

Not long ago, Steven made an appointment to see the doctor because he'd been feeling lethargic and depressed for no good reason (although, as he commented wryly, 'your sister-in-law would try the patience of a saint').

He'd expected Malcolm to test his blood pressure, ask a string of pertinent questions, even possibly send him for tests. In fact, he told him to take off his shoes and hop on the scales. Afterwards, while Steven relaced his shoes, Malcolm turned his chair so he could look out over the garden. Steven returned to the patient's chair and waited. Several minutes passed. He coughed politely and Malcolm swivelled his chair back to face him.

"Steven, how old are you?"

"Forty-six."

"You lucky so-and-so."

"What's so lucky about being forty-six?"

"How about, another ten years before you hit fifty-six?" Malcolm clasped his hands together on the desk. It seemed for a minute that he was about to say something of extreme importance about his patient's health. Eagerly, Steven leant forward.

"You need to take a bigger bite of the apple of life."

My brother was furious. "Is that it? Your diagnosis?"

"Yes it is," Malcolm said, as seriously as if he'd been telling him that it was vital he cut cholesterol from his diet.

Steven got to his feet, almost knocking the chair over in his anger. "We'd all like to take a bigger bite of life's bloody apple," he snarled, "but we don't all have the wherewithal to do it."

Apparently Malcolm said, "It's not about wherewithal," but by then Steven was heading out of the room.

Gardening is both my hobby and my work; the cinema is my passion. When I talk about the film moments I remember and relish, I light up. I become a different person.

The way James Cagney used the back of his head and the creases across his jacket to speak for him when he finally relinquished Doris Day in *Love Me or Leave Me*; Rutger Hauer as the doomed replicant in the 'like tears in the rain' scene from *Blade Runner*. I'm in the seven percent of the population who go to the cinema twice or more each week. And so a form of conversation developed with first Avril and then Malcolm that began with Avril politely enquiring, "Well, what have you been up to this weekend?" and grew over several months to become an enthusiastic, "Maggie, did you see *The Hours*? What was it like? I read mixed reviews. We almost decided to go but then at the last minute..." Malcolm, if he was between patients, strolled out into the garden and joined in the discussion. If the weather was bad we'd adjourn for a tea break in the kitchen. We pitted old films against the new, talked of directors we admired, directors we deplored, film stars we'd adored, was there any such thing as a film star any more?

Once upon a time, they'd both loved going to the cinema and then slowly they'd let the habit drop. Avril said, "Oh we began to feel there wasn't a modern film worth seeing. If we were really keen we got it out on DVD," and then her brow would furrow as if thinking back in search of the real reason. One afternoon, during my second summer working for them, she said out of the blue, "That's what it was: we both got tired of all those young faces."

I had my back to her as I deadheaded a line of standard roses. As I neared Avril's deckchair, she called out, "Oh for pete's sake, Maggie, stop and talk for five minutes. You look absolutely baking hot. Cold drink?"

I did stop. Sat down on the grass and waited while she went indoors. She came out of the kitchen door at exactly the same time that Malcolm stepped from his surgery into the garden. "Thank god," he said, "That's the last of today's."

Avril handed me a glass of homemade lemonade and fell back into her deckchair. Malcolm sat on the grass on the other side of her. He tried to close his hand around her ankle. His fingers couldn't quite meet his thumb and he frowned slightly as if surprised.

Avril said, "I was just about to explain to Maggie why we don't go to the cinema any more."

"Why don't we?" he asked cheerfully.

"Because we don't enjoy looking at all those young faces."

He laughed. "No, I suppose we don't."

Although he'd laughed, he didn't sound quite convinced. He looked at me. "Do young faces bother you, Maggie?"

"No. Not really. Not always. Not enough."

And we all laughed.

I let Avril change the subject. I sensed that they were both upset. No, nothing quite that serious. Disturbed. As if for a moment they'd glimpsed their naked reflections in an unexpectedly placed mirror.

My gardening days were Mondays, Wednesdays and Fridays. It was an enormous garden, always plenty to do. The following Wednesday it rained. A continuous downpour. Malcolm telephoned me early to say that as the forecast was dire and he had a rare free morning, perhaps we could discuss the new layout of the bottom flowerbed. He wanted to make of it a green and pleasant shield between the view from his house and the relatively new estate of executive houses.

I went over at ten and we sat with his plans and tear sheets spread out on the kitchen table. We made lists or he dictated while I wrote. It was a friendly morning with Avril in the background doing what she called 'low-level cooking', which covered bread, pastry and soups for the freezer. Outside the rain fell, the sky was a deep grey; I envied their... security.

We broke for lunch. Leek and potato soup and warm, crusty new bread. I'd almost finished my soup when I realised they'd hardly started, that in fact they were both watching me with friendly amusement.

"We've got a favour to ask you," Malcolm said.

I lowered my spoon.

"Now, if we're invading your space, don't be afraid to say," Avril said.

"Maggie, would you take us to the cinema with you?

Whichever film you want. We don't mind. Just to get us started again."

This doesn't happen often but my eyes filled with tears.

"Oh god, is it that dreadful an idea?" Malcolm said. "Avril, a piece of towel roll."

I dabbed my eyes and smiled. "No, it's a good idea. Take no notice of me."

They assumed that somehow I was overwhelmed. That because I was alone, I was lonely. But my real reason for tears was that, for a moment, I was touched by how young and eager their faces had both looked.

Our cinema-going began with much good humour and optimism. With me sitting in between them, Avril could stand those young faces on the screen, even get involved in their fictional lives. She began to relax, to allow the story and any prevailing emotion to take over. The young female stars no longer had to represent the enemy.

The change in Malcolm was less straightforward. He was interested and animated by the experience of visiting a cinema, going to a restaurant for a meal before the film. For a few hours each week he stopped being Doctor Chapman. Quite apart from the film, he observed the audience, the cinema and restaurant staff, with a sort of hungry curiosity.

This disruption to their routine inspired them both to try other things: they took up ballroom dancing, they went to the theatre, an outdoor concert in the grounds of the nearby Botanical Gardens. They seemed happier and younger. Malcolm talked more, made both of us laugh. He wasn't quite so absorbed in his garden.

But what works for me, or worked for Avril, won't necessarily work for everyone. It worked for Malcolm only for a time.

*

Six months before I moved, I saw him in London. One of those odd encounters when you meet someone you know entirely out of context. It was a beautiful spring day in late April. I was meandering just for the pleasure of meandering, to meet an old school friend and take in an exhibition of film stills at the National Portrait Gallery. I remember looking up at the sky – a remnant of bright blue trapped between the curved roof of the Brunswick Centre and the jagged outline of the Crest Hotel. Someone brushed past me. There was a fleeting impression of white shirtsleeves rolled up on tanned arms, and of the person being someone I knew. I looked back. He looked back. It was Malcolm, already about twenty feet away. There wasn't time for me to form a greeting because he raised his hand – more like he was brushing me away than an acknowledgment – and off he hurried into the Brunswick Centre.

I'd never seen him walking so fast, not necessarily with purpose but as if to be moving at speed was essential. I thought of the White Rabbit in *Alice*: "Oh dear! Oh dear! I shall be too late!" And the expression on Malcolm's face... I ticked off what I'd glimpsed: desperation, determination, and yes, an almost manic glee. Should I follow him? But then I reasoned that might be the very thing he'd expect me to do. But I was curious. I took a left turn into Bernard Street and walked briskly round to the back of the Brunswick, coming in via Coram Fields. There was Malcolm standing outside the Renoir Cinema in what seemed like urgent conversation with a young woman.

I stood behind a concrete pillar and watched. They made an incongruous couple, if that's what they were. Malcolm in his uniform of shirt and cord trousers, the woman in an ethnic blouse and peasant skirt, on her head a faded, embroidered skull cap. Long dark hair hid her face but I knew she must be pretty.

Against their drab, concrete backdrop, she resembled a colourful butterfly, very slender, very fragile. Malcolm was looking at her so intensely, it was obvious that he knew her well. Once he tried to take her hand and she slapped him away.

"No, no, no," she said.

Quite distinctly I heard his reply: "Ruth, please... you're breaking my heart."

The following Monday I mowed their lawn. It took at least an hour and was strenuous work, as Malcolm refused to buy an electric mower. He said the best results were achieved with a hand mower and I was reluctantly inclined to think he was right. It was a pensive afternoon on my part. Avril was out shopping for most of it and Malcolm doing paperwork in the surgery. As always his doors stood open. I could see him quite clearly, sometimes looking out, sometimes with his back to the garden typing up notes. I was sure our encounter must be on his mind. I expected an explanation. Any explanation. *Well, what a coincidence – fancy bumping into you so far from home. Sorry I couldn't stop, meeting a colleague for lunch.*

Finally, when Avril came back, he appeared, mooched across the lawn, his hands in his pockets. "Maggie, you have been working hard. Avril, break out extra biscuit rations," he said, smiling at me.

I couldn't help smiling back. He possessed a beguilingly warm smile.

The day I moved to the coast, Avril drove me down ahead of the removal lorry. She spent a couple of days helping to get the new house straight. We mentioned Malcolm lightly, his frustration with the new gardener, a holiday they were planning in Spain.

After that I didn't expect to see them both again. I thought because of distance and their mixed feelings about having friends they'd let the connection drop; however, one Sunday morning they arrived to spend the day with me.

Malcolm drove. He seemed tense as if the drive into places unknown had unsettled him. They brought wine and Avril's homemade bread; Malcolm carried in pots of the tall, purple verbena I'd particularly admired in his garden.

After lunch I took them down to the beach to see the small fishing fleet. It was a beautiful day. People walked on the shingle alone and in groups as they must have walked on a sunny Sunday for decades, if not centuries.

The fishing fleet never fails to move me. It's shabby and vulnerable in its smallness. The boats lie beached at drunken angles on the pebbles, their paintwork blistered, names worn away. They're surrounded by ropes, broken lobster pots, oil drums and rusting machinery. Flocks of herring gulls hover angrily, diving to snatch up a crab claw or sliver of fish.

When I see things I love, I want to share them, to say, "Look at this. Feel it, smell it, breathe in how special this is." Sometimes I misjudge my audience. They don't want to feel, smell or breathe in my offering because they have their own different treasures. I thought I'd misjudged Malcolm. Suddenly the scene seemed shabby and poor. He and Avril looked quite the opposite. Had they been boats, they'd have been luxury yachts. In honour of a sea-going day, Malcolm wore pressed denim jeans I'd never seen before, an expensive jumper and a well-cut tweed jacket. He didn't match the beach, the boats, the Sunday promenaders. His normally good-natured features were screwed up into an expression near to pain, in which I read distaste. He looked at me and Avril as if we represented an enemy and then he stuffed his hands into his jacket pockets and strode off, picking his way between the detritus and rope lines strung between the boats.

"Let him be," Avril said, "He's been very moody lately. Actually, Maggie, I think it's rather nice down here."

She and I strolled to the water's edge. It was a gentle sea, lapping against the stones with a shushing sound. Avril turned and looked up at the cliff tops and then overhead to the blue sky. "And you're happy," she asserted rather than asked.

"Very."

"We miss you. Malcolm's interest in the garden has quite vanished. I'm wondering if it will ever come back... Hello darling, had a nice walk?" she called out as Malcolm scrunched towards us over the shingle.

He ignored her and stood glowering at the sea. From the line of his jacket, I could see that his hands were pushing fiercely down inside his pockets as if an internal battle was going on. Avril noticed too.

I said, "Malcolm, I don't mind – I know the place is rather tatty and not your sort of place, but it suits me."

"Of course he loves it."

"He doesn't have to."

Malcolm still wouldn't look at us and suddenly I thought, incredulously, *in a minute he's going to cry.*

He said gruffly, "I don't know why you should say that. There's a charm. I think you made a wise choice. I envy you."

Avril slipped her arm through his. "Darling, when you retire we could always move to the seaside."

"We could – but we won't," he said.

I bag up the leaves. It is satisfying work. Order from colourful chaos. The afternoon is drawing in and there is that wonderful effect of evening mist merged with bonfire smoke from a neighbour's garden. The world is grey and slightly damp. From inside my house I hear the telephone ringing. Let it ring.

Elsie and Sprog

In a hollow of mud tucked under the root of a dead tree, something the size of a tyre lies curled into a tight ball. It is huge – for a millipede. The click of Jessie's camera doesn't wake it and she wonders if it is dead. She takes a step closer and a foul warning smell drifts out of the hollow. It isn't dead. It knows she is there.

The air in front of her has become tangible, as if a barrier has dropped out of the sky to protect her. The millipede starts to unwind its body, each segment giving birth to another, and another. Jessie has a memory of the yoga class she took in her twenties, the tensing and relaxing of limbs, unravelling her vertebrae as near as possible, one vertebra at a time.

Although the millipede is at least five hundred times its normal size, Jessie recognises it from the glossy pewter colouring of its skeletal plate. It is a Black Snake Millipede, *Tachypodoiulus niger*.

While the protective barrier appears to hold, she takes several more photographs. The millipede continues with its preparations. On each segment are two pairs of legs, each leg the size of her middle finger. They flex and shiver and then suddenly, as if a breeze is moving through a fringe of tassels, the millipede flows out of the hollow. It is no more than fifteen feet away from her. The feelers on what she takes to be its head twitch in her direction.

Jessie's first camera had belonged to her dad – a box camera he'd bought during the war. She was six when he taught her how to hold it against her stomach and look down into the square liquid eye of the viewfinder, and then when focused to click the lever at the side with her thumb. Her dad said he liked the sound the shutter made; it was like the blade dropping in a tiny guillotine. She had no idea what a guillotine was but she too liked that sound.

She'd never wanted to take photographs of people or animals. Right from the start she was interested in insects: a patch of dried grass, a ladybird or an ant, a spider or an aphid. All that was needed was for her to be patient and still. She didn't mind waiting for the complete world in the viewfinder to pause, because she knew it would – eventually.

There *were* times when for a moment she thought she'd like to catch a particular look on her dad's face, as he stood in the garden or at their gate, as if expecting a visitor. So few people passed their house. He wouldn't have liked her catching that look. There were no looks of her mother's she wanted to capture. Her mother had no secret self. With Jessie, she was always strong and as loving as such a reserved woman was able to be.

She wonders if she should say something. Make a soothing noise, the sort her cat likes; a cross between a low trill and a human purr. She realises how quiet it is and that the birds have stopped singing. When she first entered the wood... but that seemed to be part of another day: a day when the birds hadn't stopped singing and she glimpsed shapes of blue sky, like irregular jigsaw pieces through the leafy branches of the trees.

A shiver runs through the millipede's many legs and the back third of its body ripples towards her. Then the front third does likewise, its feelers down like the lowered horns of a bull about to charge. The barrier between them is gone. Pincer-like, the millipede dances forwards, its fringe of legs undulating like a Mexican wave.

She isn't exactly frightened, more fascinated. She reasons that surely it can do no more damage than the menace contained in a nightmare. A tree is at her back. A living tree. A silver birch. It is like leaning against her mother.

A year after Jessie was born, they moved from Coventry to a cottage on the edge of a village, where her father got work with a local farmer.

"I can do better than this," he told Jessie's mother.

"I'd rather you didn't try. This is all we need. Here we can be self-sufficient."

"But Elsie, I'm used to people."

"Get unused to them."

"Why should I?"

"Why shouldn't you?"

As Jessie grew up, the rhythm of their arguments was in her head every day without fail, the words forming lines of a poem that would never be finished. And at night, after the lights were switched off, her parents' low voices persisted in the bedroom next to hers.

"I want you."

"I don't want *you.*"

"When will you want me?"

"Jessie, are you asleep?" Her mother calling out.

"Never mind about Jessie. When will *you* want me?"

"When *you* don't want me."

Their bed creaking as Jessie's mother got up.

"Elsie, don't go."

"I'm checking on our daughter."

The tension in the cottage often made Jessie physically sick. Some afternoons she'd feel her stomach tightening and her head beginning to throb. Her mother always noticed just in time. "Jeff, put out the stool," she'd say.

In the scullery, Jessie knelt on the stool as she vomited into the stone sink. As she retched, she was aware of the hardness of the wood under her bony knees, and her mother's hand stroking her neck.

There were other days when she knew that both her parents were acutely aware of each other. It was as if the fine threads holding them together had inexplicably tightened. She remembered watching her mother peg sheets on the washing line, her arms raised, her fair hair blowing off her face. She remembered her dad turning away from their gate, where he'd been looking wistfully towards the village for over an hour, and saying, "Shall we hang up the gloves for an afternoon, Elsie? Call a truce?"

Unsmilingly, Elsie nodded. To Jessie, she said, "Better make yourself scarce."

Jessie took her camera and went into the woods. Afterwards, at home, they both seemed... not happy, but quieter.

With unbelievable speed, the millipede closes on her with determination, as if it has come from much further away, has been making its journey – rushing in curves over roots and dead leaves – for years, its sole objective to reach her. She shuts her eyes. The image of a giant insect alters. It is a black rope flying forward, its velocity taking it off the ground. She tries to think of other things and thinks instead that if she hadn't been thinking of other things that morning, she might have heard all the birds in the wood take flight and been warned.

For her tenth birthday they gave her a Kodak Instamatic, the two of them standing side by side in the sitting room, looking very pleased with themselves – Dad grinning and warmth in her mother's eyes.

"What do you think, Jessie?" her dad asked. "Better than that old box camera. Got its own leather carrying case."

She didn't know quite what she thought. It was like expecting her to compare a crab apple to a peach. The new camera was light and fitted compactly into her hand. She had read about them in the newspaper. They would revolutionise picture-taking. Simple to use, easy to carry about. A pocket camera. She searched for the viewfinder.

"No, you hold it up to your eye and look through." Her dad took it off her and squinted into the camera. "It's got a socket on the top for flash cubes. Smile, Jessie."

She is pinned against the tree trunk. The millipede's body coils tightly around her, around her slender neck. Its legs flutter against her skin. Not an unpleasant pressure as long as she doesn't think clearly about what is happening to her. With her eyes shut, she can tolerate – anything. She can reason that eventually the millipede's attention will be distracted and it will slip away. Or will it choke her? Will black shreds like tattered flags fly across her vision?

Something tickles her face. She experiences a sucking sensation against her cheek. *It is tasting me*. She feels something nuzzling into her hair, the sucking sensation again. Legs stroking her face as they swarm upwards over her. It goes on for a long time. Behind her closed lids, she imagines them as fingers; healthy, playful fingers. Out of childhood she conjures up her mother's voice: *This little piggy went to market, this little piggy stayed at home...*

She didn't smile but he took the picture anyway.

"Now, one for the album, eh? Elsie and sprog, summer 1963."

"No thank you," her mother said.

"Go on. That apron suits you." And he roared with laughter.

"Very funny."

Her mother stood next to her and held her hand. "Just because he tells you to smile, doesn't mean you have to," she said.

"Oh come on now. A big smile from the both of you."

Neither smiled. He took the photo but his good humour had gone.

"You're a miserable pair." He had that look on his face, as if tears were boiling up behind his blue eyes.

"You don't have to stick around, if you don't want to."

"Don't I, Elsie?"

"Enough of that. Come on Jeff, give her back her camera."

"Don't worry. I'm not running off with it. Catch."

The camera sailed into the air. There was no way Jessie could have caught it. It hit the top of the sideboard, bounced off the windowsill, and landed in pieces on the carpet. There was a split second of silence, then her dad shouted, "You bloody Useless Eustace, why didn't you jump for it?"

"You're the useless one," her mother shouted back. "No, you're not really useless. You wanted it broken. To vent your bad temper on your own daughter. On her birthday."

Jessie left them. In the hall she grabbed her jacket and her box camera. As she ran across the field towards the wood, she pictured her father leaning backwards, trying to bluff his way out of being in the wrong; her mother crouched as if ready to spring. She went deep into the wood. Behind her, she thought she heard her mother calling, but no. Her thoughts, like swarms of tiny flies, began to disperse, her breathing slowed. She hunkered down and positioned her camera.

Above her head she hears the rustle of leaves. Not a breeze, a *something* making its way upwards through the pale green foliage. With a flick of its tail that catches the tip of her nose, the millipede leaves her. She takes a step away from the tree and then another. She turns and looks up. It is still there, twenty feet above, coiled around a branch, neck craned as if trying to get a better look at her.

"I'm going now," she says.

She leaves the wood and follows the lane back to the cottage. She remembers her mother coming out to meet her, on the afternoon of her tenth birthday. Her eyes were red and one of Jessie's dad's handkerchiefs was balled in her hand.

"He's dead," she said.

"Who's dead?"

"Your dad."

"He can't be."

"I know he can't be, but as far as you or I are concerned, he is. It will be better, just the two of us."

Behind her mother's head, Jessie saw her dad on the far side of the next corn field. He was heading for the village, a suitcase in one hand, his jacket slung over his shoulder. She positioned her camera and looked down into the viewfinder. Her dad was nothing more than a tiny black insect crossing a yellow background. She didn't wait for the insect to pause, for its world to grow still – she took the picture.

Our Special Place

I head for our special place. Years ago Uncle Joe marked the route with his penknife; years later Mum marked it out again with a potato peeler. When Mum died I took over. Aunty isn't the type of woman to easily mark trees with knives. She'd cut herself. Time would be wasted and our objective lost. I have Uncle's penknife now. "Sorry trees," I say, "Just the smallest notch. It won't hurt. It hurts me more."

When I was a child, Uncle, Aunty and Mum (brother and two sisters), plus myself, lived in a top-floor flat. We didn't have a garden, so each Saturday, we walked to a wood in the Vale of Evesham for a picnic. I don't know how this routine became established but it continued unchanged for nearly ten years.

None of us bothered about the possibility of bad weather once we got into winter. Uncle said he relished a good dose of extreme weather. But in our particular chosen spot, within a dense circle of trees, in a hollow between two hills, we could hardly tell if a gale was blowing outside the wood – not so much as a tremor stirred the leaves on the woodland floor.

As we made our way out of the town I'd listen to the same conversation between Mum and Aunty.

"This is our sanctuary, our garden. While I'm alive may

they never cut down the trees," Aunty would say earnestly, as if there was every possibility that the wood would be mown down and a multi-storey car park built in its place between one Saturday and the next. Mum would answer on cue as she struggled to light a cigarette against driving rain, hail or snow, "Too right. I want to be pushing up the daisies first. Still, we must all be bloody mad – I could think of better things to do with my Saturday. "

"I love the wood," I'd chime in.

"You love too bloody much for your own good. You won't get a man with that nonsense. At the end of the day, men like down-to-earth types."

"Not once they're old and wrinkled."

"Don't cheek your mother."

"But she..." But never mind, I always went too far. Mum wasn't ever as tough and sure of herself as she acted. Jibes about age and loss of looks drew blood. Not with Aunty, who bragged that she was proud to have a face like an old torn boot: "I welcomed middle age with open arms. I could put up my feet and eat as much cake as I liked."

Once, before my time, Aunty'd had a husband, immortalised as the man incapable of opening a tin of peas. Mum didn't look for men carrying tins of peas, she'd wanted corks popping, fags lit and the air humming with possibility.

"Agnes [that's my aunt]," Mum sometimes wheedled, "What say you to the cinema instead?"

"The fresh air does us good, Dorothy [that's my mum], and anyway the girl needs exercise..."

I was 'the girl'. They both called me that and I liked it. Even now, Aunty tells the budgie, "The girl will want her tea. The girl will want a sherry. Time thee and me got the girl up to bed."

"And quite apart from the girl, Joe is expecting us," Aunty said. This in the years after Joe died.

Aunty, don't you die. Not yet. It wouldn't be fair.

"I wish, at least, you had a dog for company," Aunty said. "I worry about you, roaming around the countryside on your own."

"Don't worry. I never roam. I stick to our path."

"It will be wet," she said.

"No, it will be dry. No rain in over a week. See you later."

I kissed her cheek, tasted Johnson's talcum powder.

"Say a few words for me," she said, as she always said.

What words would she have me say? "Always in our thoughts? Gone but not forgotten?" *In a pig's eye,* Mum would have replied.

But I knew that Aunty needed her rituals, for the sake of the living; to bless us both, to ensure she saw out another year. Rituals like her *colour of sunshine, colour of sunflowers,* whenever she mentions the lime tree outside her bedroom window, which she does almost every day when I'm with her. Which makes me grit my teeth and turn my back on her, swearing that the very next time I hear her syrupy incantation it will be the last. Seconds pass and finally I answer, "Too right, Aunty," which for some historic reason is the correct and only response. Relieved, we both go away into different rooms, carry on our separate lives.

The two of us are all that remain of family. In my imagination we now watch the two of them, Mum and Uncle Joe, lounging on the opposite bank of a river. They're drinking whisky sours and smoking cigarettes. Aunty sees it differently – they've gone on ahead to check out the celestial facilities and prepare a welcome.

I think not, Aunty. In a pig's eye.

*

I live in London now. A flat with a balcony. Aunty has a tiny cottage by the side of a road that goes for miles without reaching anything interesting in either direction. She chose the road because it was nearer to the wood. The house has no garden, apart from a tiny yard at the back with her precious lime tree. That's as far as she goes now. She takes a kitchen chair and sits under the tree. She's almost housebound and has become fearful of the world outside. I visit most weeks but the pilgrimage to the wood I make only twice yearly. I have my own life – or that's what I believe until I step inside her house.

I crossed the road and climbed the wooden fence, dropping down into a field, house and aunt lost to me. A flock of fieldfares rose into the air chattering angrily. Autumn sun warmed my head and shoulders as I dawdled along the perimeter between hedge and acres of corn stubble. In recent years I've had to plan, get the walk out of the way before the burning. It wouldn't feel right to be flanked by a blackened field, aware of all the small deaths. The unnecessary violence. Aunty says I'm too sentimental to be a proper country girl, and she may be right.

"Too much of a daydreamer. Country girls are born, not made," she says, and maybe she's right again.

I look for the source of sounds; the intimate rustle of a harvest mouse, *crack-crack-crack,* as a sun spurge splits open firing seeds from its leathery pouch. In early spring I've watched two hares fight on the edge of this very corn field.

I realise my nose and ears feel cold. The sun's warmth isn't real. Only an impression. I like cold sun. Today the sun is like the silvery notes from a bell, is like a smile, is like a marching song.

I recall very little of my uncle. Any memories I have are coloured by theirs: his old tweed jacket and baggy corduroy trousers, dusty boots with grinning splits across the toes. Joe walking ahead, a bulging khaki rucksack on his back, very much the man, poking the hedgerow with his walking stick, waiting impatiently for us to catch up, his face thunderous. Next came Aunty carrying the Thermos, Mum the basket and me, the travel blanket, walking single file in our creased sou'westers.

"We were inadequate troops," Aunty says, "Joe was never in the war. Poor eyesight. I think he compensated. We didn't mind."

Out of the field and it's downhill through meadow grass. Here the hedge looks splendid, the colours – livid citrus green, glossy hop brown and the final fire of sorrel with its crimson leaves. The colours stir me up until I'm almost running, Joe's old rucksack thumping me pleasantly on the back, beating out, *Well done, the girl. Keep up the pace.*

And I'm inside the wood. We've never met anyone in here. No men with dogs or courting couples. It's off the beaten track. One day a road may be built, but for the time being it still belongs to us. Sunlight filters through the almost bare branches in wide dusty beams like strobe lights, encompassing tiny flies and frantic, soft-winged moths. It's so quiet. There's birdsong coming from far away and the remaining leaves fall in sudden silent showers of gold. I imagine I can see as far as the far side of the wood. I know this isn't true, it's a trick. In the past we've walked as far as we thought we could see and the same formation of trees stretched out again in front of us. Somehow the trees railroad us, at the very moment triumphant smiles creep across our faces – *This time we've done it* – but this time we haven't. Out we come, right or left of the wood, never on the other side; and when we've begun on the other side, out we come left or right. *We'll damn well do it next time.*

Only this is a next time and there is no 'we'.

I believe our notches in the muddy bark of the tree trunks are invisible to other eyes. They lead me to a clearing the size of a largish room, about twenty feet by twenty. My heart is slowing. I'm calming down. All remains in order. Here I am at last and there in the sunlight *they* are – asleep, hands folded quietly across their chests. Each to their own leafy sarcophagus. They lie like ancient royalty. Through the rotting leaves, I see their shapes and feel their peace that only inactivity brings. Their cerebral selves aren't here with them. This is how they rarely were in life.

The burial mounds are sited at the base of a lone silver birch tree. Before Mum and Joe died, they made their choice. Joe first, just before his heart attack, about twenty years ago. Then one afternoon out of the blue Mum said, "When I go, I'll keep the bugger company. He hates the dark."

Mum knew she'd be next, that Aunty, as frail as she looked, was the stronger. Aunty has chosen her tree, a perfect tree with a perfect crown. She looks to me to give some grandeur to her death – a lightness, an easing away. Not for her, mud beating on the lid of her coffin or being reduced by fire to a pepperpot of ashes.

From each grave, a doll's head protrudes forlornly above the leaves. Both wear red Dutch caps Aunty made from scraps of felt. How jaunty and cheerful they looked in the spring. *Don't worry about the pair of us, we'll have a whale of a time,* they seemed to be saying. Their ruddy complexions have changed to grey, faces streaked with mud, the hats are dirty and falling apart. This is when I wish for a dog, a rough-coated terrier snapping at flies and trying to distract me, when I wonder how I'll manage when Aunty dies and who, if anyone, will manage me.

The dolls come easily from their beds. Their underclothes have almost rotted away. Gently I lay them next to the rucksack and start piling fresh leaves onto the graves. My aim is to make for Mum and Joe a gold caparison fit for a king and queen. All the while I can't stop muttering, "We remember, we remember," trying to visualise a Joe who wished he'd gone to war and a Mum desperate to dance, when all her friends wanted to do was talk about their grandchildren.

I heap the leaves at least a further foot higher. They'll compress down over the coming winter. I take my time. I couldn't be more caring. Even if Joe was almost a stranger to me, he was loved by those I love.

I have my water bottle of soapy detergent and I bathe the dolls until they are spotless and some of the rose returns to their cheeks. Fresh underwear. Aunty, unlike Mum, is a stickler for personal hygiene. 'Out of sight, out of mind' is not an adage she adheres to. New hats, blue this time, buttoning under their chins with a black jet button. I return the dolls to their beds, tuck more leaves around them. They face each other. It's a remarkably convivial scene.

At this time of the year, the sun won't last much longer, so I spread out my waterproof between the two mounds and sit. The dolls watch me and I also watch, take time to reflect.

"Say a few words for me."

Because I knew she'd ask this and because I want to do my duty to the absolute best of my ability, I've spent some time finding a few words. I begin to recite one of Shakespeare's sonnets that I came across many months ago:

"That time of year thou mayst in me behold

When yellow leaves, or none, or few do hang

Upon these boughs..."

It's no good. My voice is too loud and jarring. I see Joe's thunderous brow, I hear Mum's cigarette-rough voice: "For pete's sake, tell the girl to pipe down."

I pipe down. Really there are no words worth saying; instead I think, "Mum, Joe, you both look glorious."

Aunty is watching from the window as I climb back over the fence. She is at the front door before I've crossed the road.

"I see you did get wet," she says. "Stand on the newspaper to take off your shoes."

"Yes, you were right. It's wet down by the stream."

Later, in the hiatus between finishing tea and switching on the television, she says, "Of course, you're bound to laugh."

"Try me."

She makes a production of getting comfortable in her favourite armchair, smoothing seat cover, patting cushions and rearranging crocheted chair back.

At last she says, "Now, where was I?"

"I'm bound to laugh."

"Well, you probably will laugh, but this morning while lying in bed thinking of your mother and how it was this time almost to the day, three years ago, she died..." Aunty lifted her slippered feet up to the fire. Must buy her a new pair of slippers, her stockinged toes peep through the tartan weave... "And the lime tree's leaves still sparkling away so late in the year – the colour of sunshine, colour of sunflowers."

"Aunty, spare me, I've had my fill of leaves and trees today."

"I put up with all your fads and fancies. I won't be around for much longer."

"Too right. All right? Get on with it."

She leans forward, eyes sharp and bright as my imaginary terrier. "I saw a pure white dove fluttering in the lime tree's topmost branches as if it were trying to attract my attention. I thought, *Blowed if that isn't Dorothy, saying she's well and not to worry.*"

These are the moments when I need space between myself and her. Automatically my mouth opens to say, *Mum is hardly likely to turn up as a pure white dove. She was anything but.* I stop myself. Slowly my mouth closes. Why spoil it for her? As I ask myself that question, a vision of Mum as a pure white dove seems almost possible.

Aunty sits back in her chair, such an expression of pleased triumph on her face. "There, you see," she says, "and another thing..."

"Aunty, I don't want to know."

"I didn't tell you at the time, you were only a child, but when your Uncle Joe died, I had a dream that he was floating on an air current in a bright blue sky. I said, *Joe what the devil are you doing up there?* Guess what he said?"

"Tell me."

"He said, *Agnes, the view from up here's marvellous. Bloody marvellous.*"

The Holiday Let

"I don't know about those bows," Pat said.

"They're a honeymoon couple," I said, "bows are romantic." It had taken me over an hour to tie and position the three bows and I was rather proud of the effect.

"Bows are bows," Pat said firmly, "and frankly, Lorna, nobody these days has bows tied to their headboards."

Pat's new girlfriend, a squirrel-like personage called Devonia, chittered some squirrel-like remark that only Pat could translate. "Devonia says as far as she knows, nobody ever did."

I gave Devonia my best steely glare. Couldn't catch her eye – she was off scrutinising the skirting boards in search of muesli-like dust. Felt urgent need to take Pat aside and say, "You've picked a rum one there," but no opportunity.

"What time's this lot due?" Pat asked.

I looked at my watch. "Fifteen minutes."

"Well, I wish you luck, hope they're better than the Toronto nuns."

Devonia shouted something at us from over by the window and Pat nodded and said, "You're quite right, Devonia, they couldn't be worse."

Devonia stretched out on the newly made bed and bounced her hips up and down several times, then saw how far she could stretch both arms.

"Pat, could you take Devonia home now?" I said – and she did, Devonia smirking and Pat looking aggrieved. I knew they'd discuss me later: "Lorna didn't used to be such a misery guts – it's being dumped that's done it." They'd be right.

I smoothed the Laura Ashley duvet, adjusted one errant tulip that refused to stand shoulder to shoulder with its sisters and made a final tour of my flat. All was in order: fresh towels in the bathroom, my Baby Belling cooker spotless, another small posy of flowers in a jug on the kitchen table. In the sitting room I plumped up the sofa cushions for the third time and looked out of the window. Road empty, apart from Mr E, my left-hand neighbour. Loved Mr E dearly, had known him most of my life, but couldn't prevent uncharitable thoughts creeping in – as in, wish he would either stay in his back garden or at least develop a minor illness that kept him indoors. As generous spirited and rabbit loving as Mr E was, he let Duxford Road down with his open-toed shoes that hadn't been open-toed when bought several years earlier, his ancient baggy trousers and rope-tie waist, the Grateful Dead tee-shirt which he'd found in the hedge the previous autumn and worn on and off ever since.

I realise, on the page, you may be picturing a man making a firm retro fashion statement – this is not the case. Sartorially Mr E is a mess. Also, he always has a splintered yard broom about his person and whiffs of rotting vegetables from his sorties for rotting veg to feed Alfred the Great, his giant albino rabbit, plus a dozen other flat-eared, grey-furred, twitching-nosed cronies.

Thinks: why are all my friends so unpromising? Why do they all have an affinity with animals? There's Pat and her squirrel girlfriend plus Henry the goldfish, my brother David and his wife Julie and their horses and koi carp – the latter I'm supposed to be keeping an eye on while they're in America on a work exchange scheme (not always easy to keep an eye on koi carp) – and of course there is my ex, Kate, who fell in love with Tina's clumber spaniel, Poppy, and then fell in love with Tina.

So, nobody resembling honeymoon couple Barbara and Sadie in the road as yet. Mr E saluted me with his broom and I gave him a very small smile in return as if I was sucking on a piece of lime. Found myself forced to think of Kate. This letting business had been her bright idea to distract me from the trauma of our break-up. "You could live in your brother's flat downstairs while he and Julie are in America and rent out yours. Millions of women would jump at the chance of a holiday in Stoke Newington – it's the lesbian capital of the western world. It will fill the gap of my leaving. You do understand?" Kate taking me by one reluctant shoulder and trying not to look pleased at the thought of leaving me at last. "About me and Tina? And Poppy? I would die for that dog. She's made me realise a great truth about myself – I'm a canine person and canine persons need other canine persons."

"How do you know I'm not a canine person?" I'd asked.

"Sorry Lorna, you're definitely a feline person."

"I've never had a cat."

"You've never had a dog either." She smiled as if scoring some logical point. "I promise you, you'll meet millions of women."

"I don't suppose I will."

"Trust me."

So far I'd met two women and had a telephone call from one other. On reflecting on Kate's statement, realised she hadn't specified what sort of women, i.e. intelligent, interesting etc. Sisters Louella and Marie had been the Toronto nuns. Ex-nuns, since they'd left their orders, but still liked the 'Sister' appendage. They'd insisted on sleeping on the floor and covering themselves with the rug; opened every window because they couldn't breathe in such large rooms.

"Too much oxygen, much too much oxygen," Louella gasped each time she saw me, as if I was responsible for the amount of oxygen getting into the house. They did leave behind a Rosicrucian bible and a note saying, "Dear Sister Lorna, if you ever feel a need to ask God's forgiveness, we can help."

The second couple never arrived. Or at least, they got as far as the phone box on the corner of Duxford Road, from where a Sally telephoned me to say that they didn't like the look of the area. They'd imagined Stoke Newington would be more of a village, it being mentioned in the Doomsday Book; they were really looking for the Garden of England.

However, I privately had high hopes for my honeymoon couple: Barbara and Sadie from just outside Harrogate. I'd had a long and informative handwritten letter from Barbara: "Sadie and I are looking forward to our holiday in Stoke Newington. This will be a kind of honeymoon for the two of us as we've never been able to get away together before. We can't wait for the chance to walk down your High Street hand in hand and know that we're amongst friends..." and much more. I felt I knew Barbara rather well, had a physical picture of her in my mind: an attractive, dark-haired woman of middle height – capable, a baker of bread, a reader of train timetables. I nodded approvingly at my own reflection in the hall mirror – dark hair, middle height, baker of bread and reader of train timetables – attractive, capable Lorna Tree. I would ensure that

Barbara and Sadie walked hand in hand unmolested along the High Street even if I had to march along beside them and see off any trouble.

Downstairs, the doorbell rang. I felt a twinge in the heart area. Wished Kate was with me. Don't think of Kate, she doesn't think of you. I opened the front door. "Welcome," I said.

Barbara and Sadie were not as I expected. In fact there was no Sadie, only a Barbara. Now in case you're thinking, "Oh yes, it's one of those predictable stories; Kate leaves Lorna, Sadie's done the same to boring capable Barbara, Barbara and Lorna discover a mutual taste in fine Irish linen tea towels and fall in love" – well, you'd be wrong, although I do personally appreciate a fine Irish linen tea towel.

Barbara was very tall and pale with longish black hair and heavy framed spectacles. Standing on my front step she seemed somehow to block out the daylight. My smile and fulsome "Welcome" hit her about chest level. I adjusted my head upwards and said, "Do come in." Refrained from saying, "Mind your head on the lintel/lampshade/Julie's Japanese lantern mobile," which might have been construed as 'tallist' remarks. She ducked indoors, thus missing the lintel, but did dislodge the hall lampshade and sent the Japanese lanterns flying.

"Sadie couldn't come," she said. "At the last minute her mother's feet started playing up. They do that from time to time."

Didn't know what to reply as had little in the way of feet anecdotes so said, "Feet can be very tricky."

She looked relieved and said, "Yes, they can, can't they?"

I led the way up the stairs, fighting the dip in my spirits.

Also a little unnerved, as Barbara seemed to be shadowing me as I went from room to room. Tried to get the kitchen table in between us, but no, somehow she'd nipped round behind me again and both of us were wedged between the table and Baby Belling for a moment. Had a nasty image of being suddenly pinned in a headlock: "Ok, smallfry, there's just you and me in this big empty house, no one's going to hear your screams."

"Lovely," she said, "it's a lovely flat."

I deeply regretted the bows on the headboard. I turned quickly to catch Barbara also looking at them morosely. "Lovely," she said, "it's a lovely room." Barbara in her baggy jeans and oversized check shirt was definitely not a chiffon bow sort of person, but then as Pat said that evening on the telephone, "Who is, Lorna? Name but one."

The next morning the sun shone and I set off to my job at Green Bees Fertilisers, with the intention of making sure all was ok with Barbara when I returned. Got home just after two and made my way noisily up the stairs so she'd know I was approaching – nothing worse than someone banging on your door when you're in a deep meditation or having a snooze. Rapped sensitively on the door – at first silence, then the sound of nose-blowing.

I said, "Barbara, are you all right?"

"Fine. It's all lovely," she said, her voice muffled.

"Yes, I know it's all lovely, but are you sure you're all right? Would you like a coffee out in the garden?"

"No, really. I'm reading my book. I'm having an absolutely marvellous time."

"Ok. If you change your mind, just knock at my door."

I made myself coffee and took it outside, avoiding looking up at what was now Barbara's bedroom window. Tried to act naturally, which meant I began to behave very unnaturally, adjusting the rib of my socks and whistling passages of Cilla Black songs. Did not want to be perceived as a Cilla Black fan, so switched to Joan Armatrading, whose songs aren't easy to whistle – within minutes found myself back with Cilla. Saw Mr E mucking out the rabbits on the other side of our dividing wire netting fence. Had a thought regarding Barbara being a vampire, and how you can't be too careful. Decided to have a word in Mr E's ear.

"Hello Mr E," I shouted.

"Lorna," he said without looking up.

I sidled fencewards. "Mr E," I whispered loudly.

"Lorna," he said without looking up.

"Mr E, I want a word and the word isn't 'Lorna'."

Reluctantly he laid down his shovel of rabbit detritus and gave me as much of his attention as anyone who doesn't have long floppy ears and a quivering nose gets.

"Lorna," he said.

"Mr E," I said, whispering again, "I will come out onto the patio every day around three p.m. If you don't see me for several consecutive days, will you come and investigate?"

"Yes Lorna... unless it's raining."

"No, even if it's raining, I'll be out on the patio."

"But I won't."

Two more days passed and still no sign of Barbara, although I could hear her moving around upstairs, running taps, flushing the toilet. Each day I went upstairs to see if she was ok and we had the same conversation through the closed door. She said she was fine and it was all lovely.

"But have you got enough to eat in there?"

"Plenty, thank you."

I rang Pat. "Pat, what do you think?"

"I think you're harassing the woman. Leave her alone. Perhaps she misses this Sadie. You made enough wailing and rending of clothes when Kate left."

"I did not. After the first two days I was controlled and inscrutable."

"You behaved disgracefully at my Easter brunch party."

"Only you would insist on my coming to a brunch party the day after I'd been chucked."

"Isn't that what you're doing now? Chivvying Barbara to come and have coffee on the patio with you, on the assumption that your company is better than her own or the errant Sadie's."

"Well, I'd at least appreciate a visit from you and squirrel face."

"Her name's Devonia. She looks nothing like a squirrel."

"Hamster then."

"We'll see you Saturday for breakfast, same as usual."

"I may be lying dead in a pool of congealed blood by then."

"More croissants for us in that case."

Got the Hoover out. Let Barbara sleep or fall into reflective mood with that racket in the background. I have a love/hate relationship with the Hoover; love the attachments, hate the bulky body of the Hoover that invariably hurls itself downstairs or gets lodged behind items of immovable furniture, almost as if it's saying, "You can pull that hose as hard as you like, Lorna Tree, but I'm not moving." My brother says I search out fluff for the sake of searching out fluff and yes, I must admit to a gladdening of the heart when I spot fluff. Acknowledging this made me feel somewhat dejected and a failure. Left Hoover and attachments lying in a heap in the hall and made another coffee. Almost wished Barbara would materialise and we could discuss dispiriting moments in our lives.

I decided to take Pat's advice and leave Barbara to grieve or do whatever she was doing upstairs in my flat. I kept this up for the next two days. It had become remarkably quiet above me. There was literally not a sound. Had she gone home while I'd been out at Green Bees? Had she... gulp... killed herself? I decided to leave it one more day and then immediately thought, supposing she's not quite dead? Another day could make all the difference. I knocked and called. There was no answer. Not a sound.

Went out into the back garden and stared up at the bedroom window. The curtains were open; they'd been open since she arrived. I returned to the kitchen, filled a bucket with warm water, found a cloth and a bottle of Windolene – back outside, manhandled David's ladder from behind the shed and leant it against the wall. Gingerly, because I do not like heights, I climbed up the ladder, bucket in one hand, Windolene tucked under that arm, clutching the ladder with my free hand. Ladder moved slightly and some water slopped out of the bucket and onto my trainers and the rungs of the ladder. I knew I was going to die. I saw the headline in the local paper: *Death House Claims Two Lives*. I climbed higher. My head reached the bedroom windowsill, now my chin rested on the sill and I could see in. Barbara was sitting on the edge of the bed. On the bedside table she'd positioned a mirror. She was looking at her reflection. There was something slightly different about her. I was puzzling over the difference when she suddenly looked up and straight at me. She looked surprised. I gave her an efficient, someone's got to do these jobs, sort of smile, produced my wet cloth and briskly began to wash the window. I had spotted the difference. Barbara wasn't wearing her spectacles and her hair was now tied into bunches. I recognised the ribbons from my headboard. Barbara was not dying from an overdose; in fact she looked remarkably cheerful. When I'd finished, I shouted through the glass, "Sorry about that. All part of the service. My friend Pat and her girlfriend are coming to breakfast tomorrow morning, I wondered if you'd like to come."

"That would be lovely," she said and I made my careful way down the ladder and returned it to its home behind the shed.

Saturday morning and sunshine. I set the garden chairs and table out on the patio. A few words with Alfred the Great who was munching some of Julie's dahlias through the wire netting.

"Alfred, no," I said firmly.

Alfred continued munching.

"Alfred, look, delicious dandelion leaves. Yum, yum."

He batted his white eye lashes at me and telepathised, "You eat them, then."

I meandered back to the patio to put cushions on the chairs, then into the kitchen. Dead on eleven, Pat and Devonia arrived. "I've brought croissants," Pat announced, dropping a greasy paper bag onto the work surface. Devonia mumbled something like, "Tail need eating in heaven," which translated meant, "They'll need heating in the oven," and off she scooted to check Julie's bird table for nuts.

"Is it me or has Devonia made up her own language?" I asked Pat.

"It's baby talk. She doesn't use it all the time. I think it's sweet."

"I think it's weird."

The light in the kitchen dimmed and there was Barbara, filling the kitchen doorway. I made the introductions and Pat took Barbara outside to meet squirrel chops, leaving me to make coffee and grill the croissants.

A few minutes later Pat shot back in. "I thought you said Barbara was plain," she hissed.

"I don't think I said 'plain', I think I said there was something ominous about her, quite apart from the vampire element."

"She has no vampire element. You are so non-empathetic. I tell you, I wouldn't mind having her for my lodger."

"What about Devonia?"

"I'd swap Devonia for Barbara any day of the week."

"Would you?"

"Barbara's all woman," Pat said quite loudly, with a smile in her voice. What I call, Least Likable Pat, when she's confident of a sexual conquest. She strutted out into the garden and I followed with a laden tray and a roll of paper towels tucked into my waistband.

Pat was right. This wasn't the Barbara I'd welcomed in a week ago. She wore the same baggy jeans but with a tight-fitting scarlet tee-shirt and a deep V neckline showing off a black lacy bra. She'd put on makeup, just enough to take the pallor from her complexion, to make her eyes look larger and her lips redder. Around her neck she'd tied one of the chiffon ribbons, and her thick black hair was also tied back with one. I looked meaningfully at Pat re the ribbons, but Pat wasn't looking at me, she was drooling over Barbara.

Barbara said through a mouthful of croissant, "I'm sorry I've been so unfriendly this week but actually I split up with

Sadie just before I came away. I'm still heartbroken."

She doesn't look heartbroken, I thought sourly. Hadn't affected her appetite. When I split up with Kate I certainly couldn't have managed three croissants, butter and jam, not that there had been anyone on hand to feed me bite-sized morsels. "Just another tiny bit. Must keep up your strength in times of stress," Pat was wheedling, almost sitting in Barbara's lap.

"What about Sadie's mother's feet?" I asked acidly.

"Oh, they were the reason we split up. Sadie's mother uses her feet as a weapon – and her bowels. They've ruled our lives for years."

"That's dreadful," Pat said, squeezing Barbara's thigh comfortingly.

I thought, "Pat is so obvious. I despair. What a way to treat a small furry animal like Devonia."

I looked at Devonia and smiled encouragingly. "Croissant, Devonia? Pain au choc?"

From next door I could hear the 'crunch, crunch' of Alfred as he started on another of Julie's dahlias. Devonia leant across the table and touched my hand. She said, "A lack wabbits."

I said, "Me too."

Unknown Woman with Bird and Pomegranate

I have a tradition – can I say that? I would like to think it's mine and Miss Robertson's alone, but I know it isn't – of waiting patiently. For time to pass so that there's a chance the present will become different.

From when I was a small child, Miss Robertson had lived in the house across the road. Her name made me think of Robertson's jam and once she did make me jam sandwiches although the jam may have been homemade.

Miss Robertson wore her wiry hair in a smooth French pleat as it changed over the years from brown to grey. Her face was round and pale. She had full lips, naturally pink, that looked as if they were pressing lightly against a pane of glass. Which is odd, because they often were. She was always stationed at her front downstairs window, her still figure through net curtains. Sometimes she parted the curtains and stared intently up and down the road as if expecting a visitor, but as she turned her head from left to right she'd pause just for an instant and look across at our house.

Several times I asked my mother, "Why does she keep looking out of the window?"

"Because she's got nothing better to do."

In the evening Miss Robertson switched on a pink-shaded lamp at the back of the room. Quite clearly I saw her advancing or retreating shadow. This shadow was taller than the Miss Robertson I saw outside. Outside, her shoulders were hunched and she moved very quickly as if in a hurry to get to wherever she was going and back again.

Miss Robertson's net curtains were quite plain, no polka dot or lace effect, and they were as white as it's possible for a net curtain to be. They weren't left to become stiff and grey like other net curtains in the road. Like ours for instance. Mother said this was because Miss Robertson had money. She said the Robertsons had lived in that house long before the rest of the road began to go downhill. Mother included us in the 'downhill' slide.

Once, when I was ill, Mother went into Miss Robertson's to use her telephone to call the doctor. She reported back that the house was freezing cold but fresh smelling.

"No smell of cooking hanging in the air," Mother said, "but then she's as thin as a rake – probably can't be bothered to cook, living on her own."

"What's it like inside?"

Mother shuddered, "Full of Victorian furniture. Dust traps. I used to do a bit of cleaning for Miss Robertson, before you were born."

"You never said."

"Why should I?"

After my mother died, I heard in the local shop that Miss Robertson was moving to Rye Bay. A 'For Sale' sign was up in the front garden and Miss Robertson went missing from her front window. Foolish, but I felt as if I'd been somehow held safe between the two of them and now at the age of forty-two they'd let me drop. However, one afternoon Miss Robertson knocked on my front door. She was out of breath, having struggled across the road carrying a large, heavy mirror.

"In the style of Grinling Gibbons," she said breathlessly (this meant nothing to me). "I'd always meant to give it to your mother to celebrate us both remaining 'misses'. It holds good memories." She'd smiled a lovely smile, pressing her still full, flower-like lips together. "You're very welcome to come in and have a look round, see if there's anything else you want. There won't be room in the bungalow I've bought."

I couldn't recall Miss Robertson every having said more than a few words to me in years and years, so this friendliness took me by surprise. I intended to go and 'look round' but I left it for a few days, not to seem too eager. I left it too late. On the day I intended to go, I woke to find all the curtains gone from her windows, and when I knocked on the door there was no answer. I never saw Miss Robertson again.

I thought carefully before I put up the mirror. It was quite a grand mirror with an ornate frame of carved birds and citrus fruit. When I looked closely I realised that one bird in particular was taking a peck out of what I thought might be a pomegranate. There was something cheeky about the set of the bird's head that bordered on insolent. For some reason I was reminded of my mother – or at least, my mother had often made me think of a small, bad-tempered wild bird. A woman with a permanent 'So what!?' expression on her face.

I decided to hang the mirror in the kitchen, the most unsuitable room in the house but where I spend most time during the day. I set it quite low on the wall, just above the hip-height dado rail. I work at the kitchen table, making collages from cloth, wood, found objects; now if I looked up I could see myself. My mirror reflection was like a woman in a portrait. Vermeer, say. Old fashioned, dark toned but striking.

I look what I am: a spinster who's devoted the best part of her life to an invalid mother. I don't have a cat but people assume I do. People assume I eat badly, that I neglect myself and allow the house to grow cold, adding layers of spinsterly cardigans rather than switch on the central heating. I'm nothing like this but there are days when I find myself moving slowly and awkwardly or scurrying to the shops as Miss Robertson scurried, because that's what people expect me to do.

Miss Robertson's mirror presented me with a very different set of assumptions. The reflection I saw was of a woman with an intelligent, mobile face. When she leaves the table and walks to the sink, to a cupboard or clean out of her house, this woman is strong limbed and self-sufficient. Yes, she does wear cardigans and skirts of an elderly, faded material no longer produced – that doesn't matter. The clothes are insignificant, hang like an afterthought from her body. This woman in the mirror is far too absorbed and, yes, amused by her own thoughts and plans to worry about her clothes.

I liked looking up from my work and catching my eyes in the mirror, the two of us exchanging wry smiles. We toasted each other in tea and red wine. We shared jokes, pulled faces, fussed with our hair. Sometimes we were a tussled Brigitte Bardot, sometimes we played at being maiden aunts. My reflection became my companion, but if I felt sad or anxious, I sat where my reflection couldn't see me. I didn't want to spoil what we shared; the best of us, the moments of peace when nothing was pulling at what, for want of a better word, I'll call my heart.

I'd been in Miss Robertson's house only once before, when I was five or six years old. She'd invited us for tea. Mother seemed flattered. "You're known by the company you keep," she'd told me.

I hadn't thought about this occasion in a long time but one day as I sat at the kitchen table cutting shapes from a piece of dark red felt, it appeared in my mind. I glanced at the memory almost in passing. It was like a bystander in a shabby coat, and then you focus on the bystander's face and realise you know them quite well. *I remember* – I said, then looked up expectantly at my reflection – *a dark hall.*

Several rooms led off the hall but all the doors except the last one were shut. I remember following Miss Robertson, and my mother following me, through the open door. We were in a small room at the back of the house. A circular table with a crocheted tablecloth over red felt was set out for what was then known as 'high tea'. I remember there were plates of sandwiches – jam and corned beef, cut into quarters with the crusts off. I particularly liked the jam. It was sweet with crunchy seeds in it and made the bread moist. There were jellies too: lime green and raspberry red in stemmed glasses. Was there a pink blancmange shaped like a rabbit? I looked at my reflection – *I don't think so.* Still trying to remember, I went to the bread bin and took out a packet of chocolate biscuits.

You've had enough. Remember, Mother said, "You've had enough." And to Miss Robertson, "Her eyes are bigger than her belly."

I heard this either in my head or coming out of the mirror, which common sense told me was impossible. Also I was standing by the kitchen window, at some distance from the mirror; I was no longer reflected in it. So common sense again told me it wasn't my reflection speaking and of course a mirror is inanimate. The voice had come out of my subconscious. Either theory unnerved me a little.

"I haven't had enough," I said firmly to any lingering spirit of Mother as I took the chocolate biscuits back to the table. I looked in the mirror, I looked at the piece of red felt, I ate biscuits and thought.

I remembered Miss Robertson pulling out dining chairs for us and that she and Mother almost had a tussle. Miss Robertson was trying to ease the chair forward against the back of Mother's legs while she gripped the cushioned seat with both hands and tried to take control. Miss Robertson won that round. The pressure of the chair seat forced her guest to sit. As soon as Miss Robertson let go, Mother scraped her chair away from the table defiantly – she wasn't going to be stuck with the table top pressing against her ribs.

Mother kept her coat on. And her beret, which seems odd now but not then. Women did sometimes keep their hats on when visiting people they didn't necessarily know well. She did take her gloves off and fold them into her handbag. She placed her handbag on her lap.

"Nobody's going to run off with your handbag," Miss Robertson said with amusement. Mother didn't answer. Or I don't think she did. She might have sniffed.

I wasn't wearing a coat. After all, we'd only walked across the road. I wore my best frock, a royal blue with a white collar and cuffs. Mother had bought four foot of three-inch-wide satin ribbon for me to wear as a sash, tied in a large bow at the back.

Mother and Miss Robertson hardly ate a thing. Mother said, "No thank you," several times and, "Really, I couldn't possibly." She used an affected voice and adopted mannerisms I'd never seen before, like dabbing her lips with the corner of her napkin. We didn't have napkins at home; we had paper serviettes and only used them for special occasions.

Miss Robertson passed plates and poured cups of tea. I was told to help myself but Miss Robertson inundated Mother with queries: *Tea? Sugar? One lump or two? Cream or milk? Another slice of Madeira? Not too strong? Warm enough?* almost as if throwing down challenges. Each one, Mother managed to parry. Which didn't mean she carried off her responses with aplomb, she answered in a way I see now was defensive – by refusal, by not participating. Going without sugar rather than getting to grips with the tiny silver sugar tongs, taking her tea far too strong rather than asking Miss Robertson to *please pass the milk jug.* I see now the tea party was something of a battle.

Eventually Miss Robertson turned her attention to me. She asked me questions about school, my favourite subject, if I enjoyed hockey. Mother kept silent. I imagined she was thinking, *children should be seen and not heard,* a phrase she generally used to dampen down my high spirits.

The mantel clock chimed five, which meant we'd been at Miss Robertson's house for an hour. At the fifth chime, as if it was a signal, mother took her gloves out of her handbag.

"It's been very nice," she said.

Miss Robertson looked surprised. "You're not going yet, are you, May? We haven't really talked."

I was intent on trying to finish my bowl of jelly and cream. I wasn't paying proper attention. Out of the corner of my eye I'd seen Mother reach for her gloves, although even a few minutes earlier I'd been aware at the core of me, that was linked to her, that she intended to make a move but was priming herself for it. I was thinking a whiny *do we have to go so soon?* But now in my head, like the prick of a thorn, was the name 'May'. I vaguely knew that was my mother's name.

I don't know how I knew because I'd never heard anyone use it before. How did Miss Robertson know? I looked up from my jelly, first at Miss Robertson, then at Mother. Miss Robertson was very pale, but then she was very pale complexioned anyway. Mother's cheeks had a band of colour across them. She was looking at Miss Robertson in a way I couldn't quite fathom. I'm trying to visualise her face; I think it was hostile, possibly sending out a warning.

Mother didn't answer Miss Robertson. She stood up.

"I've not quite finished," I said.

"You've had enough," Mother said – and to Miss Robertson, "Her eyes are bigger than her belly."

I remember the mirror now. It hung in Miss Robertson's hall. As we were leaving, Mother stopped in front of it and adjusted her beret. I was by the front door wondering why, if there was such a need to rush off, Mother had suddenly slowed down. Impatiently, I looked back for her. Miss Robertson stood behind my mother. Miss Robertson was about half a head taller. She was looking over Mother's shoulder into the mirror – not at herself but at Mother's reflection.

"May, you look lovely," she said and smiled.

Mother did smile back. One of her pinched, tight smiles, but still a smile.

"That's quite enough of that," she said.

Forever Argos

I didn't know I needed a bathroom mirror till Deirdre said I did.

"Your bathroom's nothing much to write home about," she said, "but a stylish mirror could give it a bit of pizzazz."

I don't spend much time in front of mirrors. When I do, they yield few surprises. My reflection is pretty much as expected, although my loss of a flat stomach sometimes still comes as a revelation and there was a time a few years ago when my jawline seemed to sag irreversibly over a mere matter of days. Basically, I'm a tall, middle-aged, mud-brown-eyed woman. Sartorially, I favour men's second-hand tweed jackets and loose corduroy trousers in any shade from moleskin to mustard.

On this particular winter's morning, I'd arranged to meet Deirdre in Debenham's. Apart from Marks & Spencer's food department, it's the only shop in Hastings that Deirdre's willing to enter. She says that although she loves the town, *per se*, it's actually full of chavs and people who smell. If she, Deirdre, won the lottery (which is unlikely as she doesn't do the lottery because that would mean going into, say, a tobacconist and possibly rubbing shoulders with chavs and smelly people) she'd go back to London and buy a three-storeyed Victorian house overlooking Islington Square.

Deirdre drives to Bluewater for most of her needs. She says, *There's everything under one roof plus fabulous eateries.* When I admitted to never having been to Bluewater she said, *Margaret, you don't know what you're missing.*

We'd agreed to meet for coffee in the Style Café. It's recently been revamped with chocolate brown leather sofas and chairs grouped invitingly. One wall is made entirely of glass so that you can look out over the promenade to the sea. I immediately spotted Deirdre; she'd bagged a table by the window but had pulled her chair round so that her back was against the sea view.

"I'm sick of sea," she said. "Don't sit down. Order the grub while I have a think about what would suit your bathroom. Suffolk sausage pie and French fries for me. And a dry white wine."

"That sounds like lunch."

"It is lunch."

"Should you?" (Deirdre worries that she may soon be classed as 'obese'.)

"I should," she said firmly.

I queued, passing the time watching Deirdre hard at work thinking while her bright blue eyes assessed the other customers. Deirdre likes to feel she's in some sort of 'top echelon', which means she has to be amongst people she thinks are like herself, in taste and buying power. Taste-wise, she allows me to be her exception, her one indulgence. Deirdre savours my lack of taste, enjoys putting me right.

When I'd asked her opinion of the mirror section in the Argos catalogue, her upper lip had quivered in a silent sneer.

"It's not a bad selection," I'd said, "There's a rather jolly porthole-shaped mirror for fourteen pounds. I've marked it with a cross."

I flicked through the pages. Deirdre laid her hand on my arm, "Don't bother. I'm really not interested. How much can you afford?"

The 'afford' question touched a nerve. I've never had much money but I don't want Deirdre knowing that. Our friendship of several years is based on Deirdre remaining forever a style guru and never losing her extraordinary sheaf of corn-blonde curls that frame a china-doll face, and the fiction that I'm a wealthy woman with at least a million and a half pounds tucked away in bonds, Isas and stocks and shares. Deirdre likes to believe that I'm one of those rich, reclusive people she reads about in the Telegraph, who die surrounded by black bin bags full of empty cat-food cartons (washed first, of course – myself as well as the cartons – Deirdre's scrupulous about personal hygiene). Oh, and she will be the sole beneficiary of this million and a half.

So I'd answered, "Whatever it costs."

"We'll drive to Bluewater."

"No, I shop in Hastings. It's every resident's duty to boost the local economy."

"Your duty apparently, booby."

So here we were in Debenham's. Lunch on me.

I was forced to complain about my own Suffolk sausage pie. It was warm, rather than piping hot.

"Suffolk pie should be warm," the female assistant said, without peeling her hips off the cappuccino machine.

"Could I speak to someone in charge?"

"Not today. She's on a course. Why not write in?"

"Why should I have to go to the bother of writing in? There can be no argument that this pie is only warm –"

I pointed at my pie, glancing over at Deirdre for support.

"Wind it up, dude," she mouthed.

"It would be cold by now," the assistant said. "Give it here. I'll bung it in the microwave."

I'd have liked to query just what sort of language 'bung it in' might be to use on a customer, but Deirdre's eyebrows had disappeared behind her fringe and she was counting the tassels on her silk scarf, a sure sign of an impending explosion. The assistant handed me back a now steaming-hot pie.

"You are a prat," Deirdre said when I finally sat down, and, "I expect you'll get food poisoning – never reheat meat – just asking for trouble. Shall we go for the lemon meringue?"

Debenham's mirror section is tucked away in the narrow corridor linking the Style Café with their china and glass department. The corridor's about twenty foot long, its wall surface only interrupted by doors for the ladies' toilet and baby-changing facilities. The wallpaper is a rusty red with a relief pattern of herons in flight. Deirdre tells me that this is a copy of an early William Morris print. I nod and look suitably impressed by her knowledge.

"Hardly cutting edge – but that's small-town mentality. Still, there's enough mirrors here to wave a stick at," she says.

"No portholes though."

"That's because portholes are common."

"I've never seen one in anybody's house."

"That's because you only know me and I'd rather swallow nitric acid than have a porthole mirror in my bathroom."

The bit about me knowing nobody wasn't strictly true. I knew far more people than Deirdre, but this was another of our pretences, that Deirdre was wildly popular.

I studied the mirrors. Wide leather frames seemed fashionable. Also a whitish coloured wood.

"Limed," Deirdre said, "but of course that look won't go with your lino tiles." She followed this with a sound, a cross between a snort and a snigger. Deirdre moved fast, inspecting and rejecting. She knew what I wanted. No, she knew what I'd want if I had any taste. Her movements were caught in the mirrors on both walls. That morning she wore a calf-length velvet coat in kingfisher blue over silky trousers and a pink shirt. Earlier as she'd bounced out of her house (in what Deirdre calls the 'salubrious Clive Vale area'), she'd apologised wryly for the pink. "I know", she said holding up her hands, "pink is so last year. I wouldn't risk it if you were a London friend."

What London friend would that be?

Of course I didn't say that. I didn't want to start our shopping expedition off on the wrong foot. (Deirdre has tiny feet for such an imposing woman. She wears pixie boots at this wintry time of year, in various jewel colours. Her hands are small as well, very white with dimpled knuckles.)

She may have known I was watching her or it could have just been what I call 'a Deirdre moment' but suddenly she began to dance. Nothing formal, just swishing her long coat around her legs and pirouetting as she admired her reflection in the different mirrors. I stood still and mute, drinking Deirdre in. (I'm not in love with Deirdre but on those rare occasions when she's not talking too much or insulting me, I find her visually fascinating.)

"Don't stare at me, chump. Look at the mirrors. That's what we're here for."

I looked at the mirrors. They were a small revelation. Their glass gleamed. Each mirror was like studying just one facet of a perfectly cut diamond. And so expensive. Even the price tags appeared to be made of faux leather.

"This is the one," exclaimed Deirdre. "Come on. Stop gawping."

I joined her. The mirror she'd chosen had no frame.

"Venetian glass. Very expensive," she said with satisfaction, "but worth it."

Etched around the edge of the mirror was a pattern of lovers' knots and roses. I looked at the price tag: two hundred and thirty pounds.

"You don't look half bad in this," Deirdre said.

Actually I looked far better than 'half bad'. I looked terrific. My eyes were a vibrant hazel colour, and yes, they sparkled with amusement. My chin seemed to have lost its companions, in fact my whole body looked svelte and athletic. I was transformed into Vita Sackville-West in her prime, or at least into the woman who'd played her on television.

"You'd have to replace all your threadbare towels," Deirdre remarked.

I saw my shabby bathroom awaiting my return, secure of its place in my affection. Yes, goodbye towels. A bathroom to match this mirror and this reflection must always have new towels in the latest fashion colours. I thought regretfully of my old chrome taps with the nickel plating showing through. Suddenly they seemed like elderly, impoverished friends. Goodbye. Goodbye, green and white lino tiles. Forgive me.

Deirdre gave me a sharp nudge, "Shove over. Let's see, me, me, me."

Deirdre's reflection joined mine. For a moment in the mirror there was an impression of much movement, as if a large ramshackle bird had flopped down beside me – a bird with flying curls and shimmering velvet sleeves – and then Deirdre became almost herself again. She studied the glass, her ready, approving smile in place. It died abruptly. She moved nearer to the mirror before stepping clumsily backwards.

"Dude," her voice was uncertain, "I don't really look like that, do I?"

Deirdre's reflection was shocking. I caught my breath. The texture of her usually porcelain skin was uneven. That china-pink foundation and powder she wears, her rose-pink blusher, appeared to be smeared on. Deirdre still looked like a china doll, but a crudely painted one. Even her corn-gold hair seemed a brassy yellow. I looked at her reflected clothes. The cuffs of the pink shirt were frayed and the hem was down on her velvet coat. On Deirdre's sleeve was a stain that was maybe gravy from her Suffolk sausage pie.

"I asked you a question."

Even her voice was different. It seemed to come out of the mirror and was as hard and sharp as the bevelled edges of the glass. I stepped back to better see the two of us. The thought popped into my head that all these years, Deirdre had been hiding behind her makeup and her clothes. I was the only one who hadn't seen it.

"I think the mirror distorts," I told her.

"But why me and not you?"

I looked at my own reflection one last time. I smiled at me and I smiled back. I'd have loved to ask Deirdre, or anybody, do I really look that good?

"I don't know, Deirdre."

She flounced out of the mirror and headed for the ladies' toilet. I moved along to China and Glass. Fifteen minutes later, when I was beginning to wonder what she was doing, I saw Deirdre marching towards me giving a dismissive toss of her head in the direction of a display of Royal Doulton figurines.

"So naff," she said, looking me straight in the eye.

She'd added more makeup and back-combed her hair. On her lapels was a fresh dusting of face powder. Would the cataracts grow back across my eyes? I thought not, yet strangely I felt the same tenderness for Deirdre that I'd always felt.

"Well," she said, "reached a decision?"

"I've decided on the Argos porthole."

For a split second she looked relieved, then her top lip rose scornfully. "Forever Argos, that's you. A regular cheapskate."

"Ah well. How about tea and a muffin in Café Revive?"

"Whatever. It's your money. Maybe a chicken wrap?"

"Should you?"

"Definitely."

Behind Glass

I never loved Jennifer. It was not her fault. When the nurse placed her in my arms, all I felt was the pull of a sinking heart. My child, my responsibility – the door to my life closing.

"You'll grow to love her," the nurse said, reading my expression.

I knew I wouldn't. She reminded me too much of her father and the struggle it had taken to inadvertently produce her. I would have chosen to forget my mistake – Jennifer made forgetfulness impossible.

Four months before her birth, he left. Said he couldn't stand it (our marriage) or me any longer. I'd embarked on the marriage during a brief period of uncertainty. Such a dangerous time, when confidence fails you – I'd grasped at anything that was offered, however far removed from my ideal. We didn't divorce. For once we were in agreement – between us, we'd expended enough energy. "Bad karma," he said, before going to live in Spain with a succession of freer spirits.

Each month he sent a small allowance. Just enough to rent a two-bedroomed house in a northern village, with a little left over to live on. He imagined its meagreness would force me out to find work, into what he termed 'a healthier environment'. Such a hypocrite. So many opinions on what was and wasn't beneficial for my human condition.

Had I found a job, I do accept our life – mine and my daughter's – could have been quite comfortable, but comfort is no replacement for losing a sense of myself, as I would have done in some chattering office. And then again, I rather liked that tentative connection via his monthly cheque. It amused me to retain a fingerhold in the world where men and women walk the earth's surface and communicate. Responsive behaviour, intermingling, cohabiting. I'm different. I cherish my own company. I stay still.

Not that I'm lazy. Although my life these days is more circumscribed, then, forty years ago, I had plenty to do. With house, garden, a child, moments I could have for my own were precious.

The house I rented was an end terrace. Its unfenced back garden drifted away into open fields while to the left of the house was a cemetery enclosed by black iron railings. Especially in spring and summer, the cemetery was an enchanted place. I loved to sit on my particular bench and listen to the murmur of insects, the birdsong and at dusk the call of owl and nightjar. There was nothing morbid or fearful, living near to the dead. Remember, this was 1963, wars and diseases were closer, death expected, almost, sooner rather than later – if not a friend, it wasn't quite the enemy it is today, held at bay whatever the cost.

Jennifer was a solemn, stolid child, which made her presence easier to tolerate. This may sound harsh but I try not to nurture any illusions about myself. I never ill-treated her. I did have to force myself to show an interest and, frankly, sometimes the effort was beyond me. I did my best.

When she was small I took her several times a week into

the cemetery. It was a safe place where she could play and leave me to dream. Then at about the age of five she made friends with a child from the house next to ours. Roxy was a pretty girl, a year older than Jennifer with a lighter touch on life. The two of them spent hours making necklaces and bracelets from wild flowers. They had an old tin jug of mine that they filled with water from the mossy tap, pouring it into the urns where flowers wilted. They pretended the flowers were poorly patients and spent long hours diagnosing ailments and concocting medicine from leaves and mud.

Long summer days spent, air sticky with the lush smell of sweet cicely, campion, wild parsley growing to enormous heights as if the dead blew nurturing breath on their roots. I was tranquil, achieved a measure of contentment – the children's voices mingled into the frieze of birdsong. I sat and smoked and made patterns in the gravel with the toe of my shoe, dreaming dreams of what might be, with no real desperation to see these dreams fulfilled.

The children began a new game, the 'invisible game': a combination of 'statues' and 'hide and seek'. Standing, crouching, keeping very very still, they would blend into the background and then whistle for me to come and find them. Jennifer was surprisingly adept at the game, inventive even. I'd hear her whistle strong and piercing and think she must be almost at my shoulder, only to eventually spot her thirty yards away. And then again the whistle – this time distant and plaintive, yet there she was, kneeling in the grass on the other side of a nearby headstone. She began choosing her clothes specifically for the game. Because she was a very careful little girl, I let her borrow cardigans and scarves from my chest of drawers in grey, olive green and black.

Roxy took the game far less seriously. She was usually the first found. A sneeze or a giggle, a billow of pink or pastel skirt, a scream if she saw a beetle. She was happy to be spotted, would far rather be seen than overlooked. To Roxy, I was the perfect mother – I let them do as they liked. Her own mother told me this, stopped me in the street, reproof in her voice. She was a loving mother, I, a careless one. She recognised that the favour I found with her daughter was unearned.

Up until the ages of eight and nine, the two of them followed me everywhere. They were eager and excitable, running this way and that like happy puppies, panting up to me with flowers or odd-shaped pebbles, a dandelion clock to blow, a four-leafed clover to wish over, singing, shouting – and silence – then a high whistle. I'd turn around and find myself alone. Nothing moved, yet everything somehow seemed to be moving in the shimmering heat. Concentrate, concentrate and yes – there they were – Roxy in a yellow dress at the edge of a field of ripe corn and finally Jennifer transfixed, dark and serious with her eyes closed, willing herself invisible against the trunk of a tree.

A summer came when I was discarded. I remember waking one morning to a silent house; Jennifer was already out playing in the fields. From my window I could see her and Roxy with some other children. I thought they were probably Roxy's friends. My Jennifer didn't seem the sort of girl to attract. At about that time I received a solicitor's letter advising me of my husband's death. I would get a widow's pension, not as much as his monthly cheque – from now on we would be forced to subsist. It seemed unnatural that he was no longer in the world, impelled each month, against his will, to think of us.

There came a difficult period of time. I own, his death

coupled with the children's defection shook me. Yes, at first I did feel odd. Bereft isn't quite the word I want. A sense of aloneness as if I was trapped inside a glass ball. I read a good deal, joined the library, preferring the one in town to our local. I know what it's like in small communities – a woman alone, speculations made, characters assassinated. Much reading, a little gardening, no time off for quiet reflection and inevitably, as has happened before, my prison cell became familiar territory and my need to beat my hands against the glass diminished.

Years passed quickly. I don't think I aged much. Any grey in my hair was carefully coloured to blend with my natural brown at my visits to the hairdresser every other month. Jennifer surprised me by becoming a personable young woman. It's an old-fashioned word, 'personable'. It very much described my daughter. She still retained a clumsy awkwardness of movement when embarrassed or shy but – to damn with faint praise – she developed a likable personality. Also she was pleasant to look at, with her bronze bell of hair and hope shining from virginal grey eyes. Never stunning, like her friend Roxy, who could electrically charge any room she stepped into. Of course I accept that I see Jennifer in the cruellest way – all the closeness of motherhood without the bias of love.

Another surprise, she found herself a boyfriend – a schoolteacher at the nearby primary school. Nothing extra special but 'a nice young man'. Isn't that what mothers hope to say? Prospects good. He may go far. She could do worse. She could indeed. Instead she bloomed, became vibrant, vivacious even. The change was extraordinary. I was silenced and fascinated. The few evenings she stayed at home during the week, she'd kiss me on the cheek, "Night-night Mum," and go up to her room as soon as we'd finished dinner. I'd hear her bedroom door shut firmly then, after a few moments, she'd switch on her sound system – Blondie, night after night – 'Heart of Glass', 'Sunday Girl'. She would have liked to look like Debbie Harry but couldn't quite bring herself to bleach her hair; Steve might not like it. I knew what she was doing up there on her own, practising makeup and pretty pouting expressions, searching out different outfits to enslave him. Finally she'd get to bed, struggling with sleep until early mornings. Sometimes in her sleep she called his name, "Steve." Innocuous enough, but harshly distorted to sound like a wild, sensual cry.

Steve this and Steve that – how she loved to use his name. Steve took her to dances, parties, out for spins in the countryside in his Mini Minor convertible. He wasn't in love, I saw that straight away. He may have had an affection for her but the passionate impetus came from my daughter. Several times I watched them from my darkened bedroom window as they embraced under the orange glow of the porch lamp – her body pushing into his, her hands drawing his hand to her breast, squeezing his fingers into her soft flesh. I thought she was a fool to give so much of herself away with so little guarantee of repayment. And he would always be the one to break free from her. He at least had the sense to recognise that he didn't quite want as much as she was offering. Off he'd go, hopping into the car almost with relief, leaving Jennifer breathing hard and staring out into the night long after the car headlights had disappeared.

In the excitement we'd both forgotten Roxy. She'd been away in London at teacher training college for almost a year. She was no longer part of our lives. From time to time I met her mother in the street and we exchanged grim nods as if at some point we'd argued irrevocably. One day she stopped me at my gate. "Roxy's coming home," she said almost gaily and I realised she was so happy to have Roxy back, she had to tell someone – even me.

"That will be nice for you," I said.

"Only for the summer holidays, but it will make a difference. You're lucky to have Jennifer. I don't relish living alone."

I'd never asked what happened to her husband. Not my place to pry. I said nothing – had nothing to say.

She flushed. "Takes all sorts," she said.

So, Roxy was coming home. Jennifer's self-absorption was breached at last – a very different state of affairs to present to her childhood friend – a 'Steve' to show off, however mediocre a 'Steve' might seem to a bright butterfly.

I expect you can see what's coming. An old, old story re-enacted. To Jennifer and myself, our faces in the mire, as it were, well, we were the last to spot the inevitable. Enter Roxy, fresh from her London year – a pretty child now become a beautiful young woman. Didn't take long for 'all change and change about' to occur. Steve meets Roxy and is dazzled, can't help his glance sliding towards her, can't help his face brightening, his posture improving at the sound of Roxy's musical voice in the next room. It was as if Steve and Jennifer had never been any more than good joshing friends – were still friends. Why, Roxy and Steve were emphatic about the depth of their affection where she was concerned. Hadn't she brought them together?

It was a sleight of hand that could have only worked on an innocent like my daughter. Increasingly, the expression in her eyes grew more bewildered, as if she'd recently learnt to swim and couldn't now understand why she was drowning. No point in further cataloguing her disintegration, but disintegrate she did.

Even I would like to believe that occasionally the underdog wins. But if they ever do then it's that rare occurrence that renders fools ever optimistic. No underdog winning here. At the end of Roxy's six-week holiday, she and Steve went back to London in his car, smiling and waving as they drove away. Roxy's mother and myself and Jennifer smiling and waving back like three trained monkeys.

Indoors, the shadows closing in on the day, Jennifer and I had nothing to say to each other. I knew how she felt, how pointless words were; I chose to continue as if nothing had occurred. One evening, a week later, I came in from the hairdresser's to find she'd gone, her suitcase and a few clothes taken. No letter.

I didn't try to find her. I intended to but each day made excuses for myself. I was paralysed. Selfishly, I kept seeing the disappointed woman Jennifer would grow into. She and me – devoted mother and daughter – only we would not be devoted, we'd be prisoners of circumstance.

That autumn, Roxy's mother moved down to London. I knew nothing until an estate agent's 'Sold' board appeared in her front garden, and by then the house was empty. At Christmas she sent me a card. Inside was a note from Roxy to Jennifer. Naturally, I read it. She apologised for any upset caused. It had been a 'spur of the moment thing' because she'd known Jen would understand. However, after only two months together they'd split up. He'd bought a little flat in Willesden Green. She enclosed his new address and telephone number in case Jennifer cared to write. "I think he'd be really glad to hear from you, Jen. We both miss you."

After Christmas I threw her mother's card away. The note with his address I kept for some time wedged under the mantelpiece clock. It looked untidy, that scrap of yellowing paper waiting to be read. One afternoon I threw it on the fire.

In the middle of a hard winter there was suddenly a phantom spring. Two blessed weeks at the end of February before the weather plunged back into rain and gales. When it had been sunny for three days in a row, I walked across to the cemetery. A new bench had been placed by the grave of a Rowena Stowell, donated in memory of a beloved wife and mother. The bench was quite dry, warmed by the weak sun. It seemed almost an irony to sit on it but sit on it I did – and spent several minutes thinking about Rowena Stowell and whether she was really so well beloved. And then my mind wandered, tempted as it always was by the different faces and smells of nature. To me, nature is a lovely woman wearing robes of green or rich brown. That day she walked among the gravestones carrying a branch of yellow forsythia in one hand, the other hand held out to catch the breeze. The air had a particular purity only ever present early in the year when winter has washed it clean. I breathed in deeply, intent on the white blue of the sky.

"Mum," the word only a whisper, "Mum."

There was Jennifer, sitting quite still on the stone steps of the church. She must have been so cold in her thin grey coat, a shapeless thing I'd never seen before. Her hair, her one lovely possession, looked lifeless and was streaked with grey.

"How are you?" I said, keeping my voice cool, almost as if I were talking to a stranger.

"I'm all right. How are you?"

"Pretty good. Happy as Larry." I lit up a cigarette. "Do you smoke nowadays?"

"No." She frowned. "Have you heard from Roxy?"

There it was, straight away. She couldn't even manage an exchange of civilities. After three silent years – first things first – expose the same needy Jennifer.

"Yes, she wrote one Christmas. She'd started teaching at a school in London as I recall," I said, letting the cigarette drop and making much of extinguishing it with the heel of my shoe. I didn't want to hear the question I knew was coming, wanted to forestall it with my brusqueness. No, no, I have better things to do than sit in the cold and answer the obvious.

"And Steve?" she asked.

I said nothing.

"And Steve, Mum? Did Roxy mention Steve?"

"Jennifer, they're both fine. Actually, they were buying a house together in Willesden Green I think – probably a couple of kids by now." I smiled – a gentle twitch of my chilled facial muscles. I would almost have liked to say, "Come home, Jennifer. What does Steve matter? Warm yourself at my fire." I said nothing. Did nothing. Inactivity has always been my only suit.

She covered her face with her hands and rocked back and forth, her loneliness, her complete isolation a palpable barrier between us. I had to... I held out my hand, which was pointless. Jennifer clambered to her feet and began moving awkwardly away from me. Within seconds her solid, grey figure had disappeared amongst the dark poplars edging the cemetery.

A small cloud dipped in front of the sun and the light changed. Sinister shadows uncurled across the gravel path to where I sat perfectly still. I knew I'd shown my hand at last. My feelings for my daughter finally manifesting into action against her. I wasn't frightened or nervous, only a little uneasy. From the dense black of the trees behind me came a high mournful whistle. I didn't move. I've never run from anyone or anything. The whistle came again. A desolate note, much closer this time.

And then silence. No birdsong, no movement in the trees, like a huge breath being held. I am a hard, unsentimental woman, but against my will a change occurred. Something, someone took my words and thoughts by the scruff of their necks and forced them to see a kind of sense.

My voice, loud in the silence, called out: "Jennifer, they did not marry. They do not have kids. I have his address. Damn it, he may even want to see you."

From the pocket of my jacket I took a small address book, its leather cover worn from where I'd turned it over and over so many times. The pages were empty except for the one address that I'd copied down three years earlier. I laid the book on the bench and walked away from it. At my gate I looked back; the book had gone.

Three times since then, as I've sat in the cemetery, I have heard her whistle. On each occasion, it was an idyllic summer's day, like those that seemed to form the sum total of her childhood.

The Passing Guest

I came across the church by accident: a small clearing in woodland, two miles from the unfamiliar town where I was staying. No road passed by, only a footpath, one person wide. A church not meant to be found.

There was nothing frightening in its solitude. The light was bright, the day sunny. Why, there was a grass lawn each side of the neat gravel path that led up to the church porch; a pretty boundary wall of painted stone. What is there to fear when you imagine a lawnmower used twice a week at that time of year, when you know that somewhere nearby a tin of white masonry paint is stored, a skin not yet formed across its creamy surface? Someone who mows and paints and stoops to pull weeds from between shiny-leafed rose bushes. What is there to fear?

I wasn't happy. I'd run from a row where all the bitterness and noise had come from me. It had bounced off Monica's indifference like so many blunt knives; the deserted church offered peace. Inside, the silence soothed me, warm as a summer sea. Sun streamed in through the plain high windows, beneath my hands was the comfort of old, smooth wood. On each side of the unadorned altar, a pew stood, each cushioned in velvet, once purple, now almost black with age.

I breathed more easily, my jarring thoughts eased; here

was a place and time to move slowly, to rest. I chose the pew in full sunlight, resting my forehead against the palm of my hand. I'm not capable of prayer. I can commune, that's all. If I closed my eyes, I felt I would for once have the space to understand my life. To see the wrong turnings taken, the right ones I'd missed. Instead I was overwhelmed with a sense of complete desolation, as if an ice-cold hand had cupped my heart. Quickly I opened my eyes back into the sunlight. The sensation disappeared, but now I was aware of sounds behind me. I could hear whispering, the rustle of cloth, the crack of dry paper, so faint I realised these sounds must have been with me since entering the church.

I left the warmth of my pew and followed the sound back towards the entrance. There was a narrow wooden door on the left-hand side. In its lock, an old brass key was moving, turning and twisting. I put my hand over it. It continued to turn. I couldn't hold it steady; the whispering grew louder, more insistent, coming from the other side of the door, hissing an eerie, unintelligible entreaty. I put my ear to the wood and imagined I felt the press of imprisoned souls. I heard the feeble scratch of nails and saw futile, bloodied hands too weak to do more.

"Please, oh please, oh please," sad, clamouring voices rising, finally falling away like a dying wind.

I did nothing. I was frightened, more than frightened. Not running, but walking fast and loudly out of the church, crunching over the gravel, desperate to distance myself from those voices, yet unready to take the dark path back through the trees.

How healing is sun and blue sky, the loud singing of blackbirds. I was safe. Ghosts and voices, the dread of lonely places – we all have our tales to tell. I decided I would take mine back to Monica's flat and we would laugh and shiver and perhaps come back together one day.

For a moment, I sat on the wall looking back at the church. I was smiling, shaky still and, for all my apparent ease, ready to run. From behind the church came the benign rattle of a lawnmower being pushed by hand. Before it came into view I could smell and savour the plumes of fresh cut grass tumbling from between the rolling blades. The gardener appeared, moving easily, khaki trousers, shirtsleeves, a lit cigarette. Not a man. A woman.

This is no love story. Any love I was capable of died before this story was born. No, this woman, as pleasant as she looked, as relieved as I was to see her, was a catalyst, no more than that.

Tall. She was my height, hair greying and short like mine. We were of similar age. She nodded an acknowledgement, mowing towards me, head bent as she concentrated on the line she was setting across the grass. When she reached the wall she stopped, turned the mower around and set it in place for the next run.

"Lovely day," I said.

"Yes, are you all right?"

"Sorry?"

"I saw you rushing out of the church. It's only mice and wind currents in there. At worst, just voices."

"And the key?"

She shrugged. "The key is the key. Some things have no explanation."

"Is the church used?" I asked.

"Well, it's not popular. Too far off the beaten track. But Easter, Harvest Festival, good-weather events, that's about all. I'm paid to keep it tidy. Tuesdays and Saturdays, April to November."

"Aren't you frightened, out here on your own?"

She smiled, a sweet, surprising smile. "We're all frightened of something. I'd better get on."

She stubbed the butt of her cigarette against the wall, then pushed it into the earth.

"What's your name?" I called.

She didn't hear me over the noise of the lawnmower.

I've said that love has no part in this story. That it had died. Not exact enough. Dying suggests a fading away, flame to ember to ash; nothing as abrupt as the reality. My love was licked up, incinerated in just one of the many bonfires Monica lit around her. From a distance I'd loved her – up close, love perished. Subservience, a distorted infatuation, was all that was left.

She was attractive, not pretty; clever, not kind; ruthless, not generous – charming when it pleased her to be. Physically, she charmed me. I might be wounded, angry, yet still I remained bewitched by her limbs, her posture, the sounds she made, however ugly – oh, the configuration of her body – lying on the floor, on her bed. 'Love,' you might call it – far too painful to be love.

I ran the last half-mile to her flat, polishing and elaborating my story like a stone not quite fine enough for a platinum ring: a story of ghosts and gardeners, or mice and wind currents; humorous, cynical – no mention of my miserable fears. Fast up three flights of uncarpeted stairs, my key twisting easily in her lock, opening the door to high, laughing voices.

Monica and her friends. She had so many. An endless stream of kettle filling and overflowing ashtrays, the telephone ringing late into the night. Only friends, yet they took up all her time, transforming my time to self-pity and destructive, jealous anger.

Her friends, her kitchen, their hands half raised in greeting, half-hearted smiles to match. Monica passing me a cup of cold tea, saying, "Watch out, everybody, I think our Sandra's about to burst. Brought her loved one back a wee scrap of news and can't wait two minutes to let it out."

The woman on her right began to laugh.

"Fuck off," I said and walked out of the room.

"Oh dearie, dearie me." Monica's mocking voice and their laughter.

Later, nice as pie again, rubbing the back of my neck gently, saying, "Come on, Sandra, a little fun, means nothing, we all tease each other. Sandra, Sandra, tell me a story."

In the dark I told her, our faces almost touching, duvet pulled up around our ears.

"On Saturday, we'll go together," she said, "the two of us. An outing. We'll investigate."

All was reconciled. She took my face and pressed it into the warm silk of her breasts, wrapped her legs around my waist, pulling me into her body. That feeling, when night surrounds you both, blotting out the conflicts of the day and you and she either drown or fly.

I was pushed forward by events. Monica, for her part, had become careless. It wasn't jealousy on my part – I'm a coward – I know it, so did she. Push a coward even an inch farther than their fears will sustain them, and be careful. Don't leave your back exposed, don't let your attention wander, not for a minute, not for a split second. Us cowards, we're forever alert, waiting for a chance to escape, to rid ourselves of our persecutors.

*

At ten o'clock the following Saturday, Monica and I set out. The morning sun was behind us, baking our shoulders and the backs of our heads. We carried small rucksacks containing sandwiches, a can of Coke each, a bottle of mineral water. Over the rusting railway bridge, we took the path that ran up into the woods. On each side we were hemmed in head-high by blackberry bushes, their thorny suckers clutching at our ankles. The blackberries were huge, hanging in lustrous clumps. I pulled several off. They were as sweet as if soaked in sugar.

"Try them, Monica, they're delicious."

"No thanks."

"It's such a waste. No one collects blackberries any more," I said.

Ahead of me, her shoulders twitched irritably.

"We could pick some on our way home," I persisted.

"I don't think so," Monica said.

The church was locked.

"I'm sure she won't be long – she said Saturday."

"Did 'she' have a name?"

"I told you, we only spoke for a moment."

Monica sat down on the grass, pulled her can of Coke from her rucksack, opened it and drank. We waited in silence. Finally I asked, "What are you thinking?"

"I hate you asking me, 'What are you thinking?'"

"Sorry."

"You do it all the time."

"Sorry."

"Sorry's not good enough."

We heard the hiss of bicycle tyres and the woman's head

and shoulders moved lazily towards us on the other side of the wall. She waved, seeming unsurprised at our being there.

"Won't be a minute," she called as she sped past. I looked at Monica. She was smiling.

Within fifteen minutes Monica had a name and a life history, mutual experiences, a synchronised childhood. I could see they would meet and talk and laugh with all her other friends long after I was gone and well forgotten.

"Sandra says she heard ghostly voices," Monica said, without looking at me.

The woman shrugged. "Ghosts. I don't know. I've heard the noises, never seen anything. It's so familiar, I hardly notice it any more. They're just the sounds of an old disused building."

"Will you show me?"

"If you want."

Monica walked into the church, up to the altar, ran her hands over the backs of the pews as I had done. It was peaceful, no wind today, no voices, no scratching of nails on wood.

The gardener unlocked the side door, leaving the brass key in the lock, and went in ahead of us. It was a small cell-like room, no furniture, nothing. A square box lined with grey stone, two triangular windows set high on the outer wall, the light from them marking the floor like the distorted eyes of a clown. On the floor, in one corner, was a worn engraving:

Hear my prayer Lord,
Listen to my cry,
Do not be deaf to my weeping,
For I find shelter with you:
I am a passing guest.

Monica knelt to read the inscription, tracing the words with her finger, while the gardener stood, arms folded, her calf almost brushing Monica's shoulder. They were a pair, confident equals. I was someone to close doors, to shut up shop.

"I'll wait outside," I said.

The gardener nodded. Monica didn't look up. I pulled the door gently closed, turned the key, left them to it. Probably I'd reached the trees before they realised. I hurried. I wanted to be out of range when they started to shout.

I believe we make our own hell. There's no point in believing in celestial punishment, teaching of lessons, all the pain, all the guilt – we cause the situation that brings about its own retribution.

I stayed on in Monica's flat and waited for her to come home. Someone would let them out, I was sure of it. I parried all questions. I said, "She's gone to London – one week – maybe two – staying with friends."

After three days I began bolting the door, imagining dragging footsteps on the stairs. Doors frightened me, opened or closed. I was fearful of letting her in, fearful of shutting her out. She had water, most of the can of Coke, sandwiches. How long could they survive if no one came? A week? Yes, at least a week. I couldn't sleep. I fell awake into nightmares. After six days I went back.

In those six days, summer had slipped into autumn. The blackberries hung in desiccated bunches, their leaves beginning to curl. I walked with my head down into driving rain, my thin tweed jacket soaked. The trees creaked and swayed, wind washing through them with huge gusty sighs.

The church door stood open, leaves banked inside the porch. I didn't go in. I stood on the threshold and listened.

I could see the narrow door, the key in the lock, unmoving. They wouldn't be dead – not in six days. Frail, mad, surely not dead.

I stepped onto the grass and went silently around to the other side of the church. I found the shed. Its door had broken from its hinges and lay across the path. There was a wooden ladder, old but sturdy, all I needed.

Not a sound except the beat of my heart to alert them. I rested the ladder against the wall. Slowly, stealthily, I climbed up towards one of the triangular windows. In the half-light I could see them, huddled together on the floor of the cell, limbs twined around one another for warmth. I imagined the smell, the horror of that tiny room; not one passing guest, but two.

It wasn't enough for me to see them like that – two heaps of grey clothing, dehumanised. I had to see their faces, their souls. I rapped on the glass; jaunty, just a fellow up a ladder saying, "Hey, break it up in there."

At first nothing, then a slow unwinding of limbs, curled bodies rolling onto their backs, like two worms poked with a stick. I saw no souls, only blurred, unrecognisable faces.

"Please, oh please, oh please," their whisper shivered through the glass.

I went back to the flat and collected my things. Only a small suitcase, not much to show for two years of my life. I disappeared back to Birmingham, did the necessary to avoid being found. Through a friend of a friend of a friend, I heard: two days after my visit to the church, a Mrs Shephard had come in to decorate the church for Harvest Festival – they were both still alive.

Impossible for me to leave matters quite there. I was

uneasy, dissatisfied. I needed something more to close the chapter. Two weeks later, from a kiosk in New Street Station, I rang Monica.

"Hello," she said. Her voice, yes, but cautious, hesitant – a change had taken place.

"It's me. Sandra," I said.

A strange sound then, choking that became crying. She didn't put the receiver down on me, she kept on, crying and crying as if her heart and spirit were broken.

Oh yes, my pain was still with me, red hot in my breast, but those tears, for whatever reason, they did me the world of good.

Life on the Slow Train

The train makes sluggish progress along the south coast towards St. Leonard's, home of Rider Haggard and me. My aunt says that this macabre name-dropping, i.e. affiliating myself and home town with the good, the great and particularly the dead, is unhealthy and should be nipped in the bud.

My aunt – no, I shall call her Aunty, which sounds more loving, less reserved – lives in Worthing. Over the last ten years she has lived in East Worthing, West Worthing and now Central Worthing. As far as I know there is no South or North Worthing. If I find out there are such areas I won't pass on this knowledge, as Aunty, although now ninety-one, is still searching for the Holy Grail of flats. The appendage of 'South' and 'North' might make her dream fresh dreams of spacious apartments filled with a white northern light, or perhaps that perfect bungalow with south-facing patio. It's the words that set her off, nothing to do with intelligent thought or common sense.

Now you can relax because nothing exciting is going to happen in this story. I'm on my way home. Knowing the cafeteria at Worthing Station will be shut, I've brought along yesterday's *Evening Standard* and a Kit Kat from Budgens. I have my notebook to jot down anything worth noting and I have time for reflection. What am I reflecting on? I'm reflecting on Aunty pooh-poohing my mention of Rider Haggard.

When I visit friends in London they are often interested in the fact that Rider Haggard lived in St. Leonard's. Rider Haggard is ok to mention these days, since films have been made of his books. Quite a cachet to bring him into a conversation. However, out on the coast, not so good.

Aunty's elderly women friends (with the exception of her cleaner, Mrs Druce, who has no time for books apart from the Bible and the Book of Common Prayer), no longer read very much but retain fond memories of books they read in the past. They have special misty smiles on their faces when they recall, "Dear John Galsworthy, Somerset Maugham, Dorothy L Sayers", some of them even harking back to GK Chesterton.

I have tried Catherine Cookson with them.

"Did you know Catherine Cookson lived in Hastings Old Town, right next door to St. Leonard's, for many years?"

"Do we know a Saint Leonard?" Aunty asks maliciously. "Somebody look up *The Lives of the Saints.*"

There are no men at these tea and book discussion gatherings. Generally the men are all dead and rarely mentioned except when the conversations turn towards death and burial. Aunty often expresses an ardent wish to go in next to Uncle when her time comes, although to go in next to him when he was alive was the last thing she wanted.

"Would my funeral be a good time to visit me?" Aunty had asked sarcastically on the telephone last Thursday. I would have liked to answer a pert "Probably", but instead replied with the incomprehensible, "Possibly, very shortly in the not too distant future," as I pulled a face of despair at the cat.

"Well, I don't suppose I've got much longer," Aunty said mournfully.

I was inclined to agree with her: "Yes, I don't suppose you have got much longer, after all you're over ninety." Instead I said, "Ok, I'll come next weekend."

"Which day?"

"Saturday. P.m. I'll bring cake, shall I?"

"Where from?" (As she's grown older she's stopped bothering with words like 'please' and 'thank you so much'.)

"Morrison's." My heart is sinking. At the point when I mentioned 'cake' I'd signed my own death warrant, although of course nothing quite so drastic.

"Well, if you're going to Morrison's..." she says.

"Yes?" I bark.

"Never mind. I can tell by your tone of voice that running an errand for me is the last thing you want to do."

(Surely I'm too old to run errands?)

"There is no tone to my voice. What do you want from Morrison's?"

"No, no. Never mind. It's obviously too much trouble... although how you expect me to manage, living as I do on the second floor and with my knees..."

"Nobody forced you to buy a second-floor flat."

"Nobody forced me? Circumstances reduced me to buying what I could afford. I certainly wouldn't choose to live in this cramped eyrie looking out onto a bus-shelter roof if I'd had the money to do otherwise."

We both sighed loudly.

"What do you want me to get?"

"I've told you, never mind."

"Aunty, what do you want me to get?" I'm now shouting into the receiver; the cat is looking worriedly at me. I try to reach to administer a comforting caress, whereupon the telephone falls off the table and she races out through the cat door, possibly permanently psychologically scarred.

"What's going on?" Aunty was also shouting.

"Nothing. I dropped the phone."

"Who dropped the phone?"

"Who do you think? I, I, I dropped the phone."

"I'll have a Battenburg cake and two boil-in-the-bag chicken stew and dumplings."

"They won't have the boil-in-the-bag."

"They will. If they haven't, they'll have them in Iceland."

"I'm nowhere near an Iceland."

"And some Edinburgh biscuits."

"This isn't Fortnum & Mason's; this is Morrison's supermarket, Hastings. I've never heard of Edinburgh biscuits."

"You'll know them when you see them. And if you're coming in the afternoon, better get a loaf of sliced white and some cream cakes."

"What about the Battenburg?"

"That's for the girls on Tuesday."

"The girls shouldn't be eating cake."

"You think you're so amusing, don't you?"

"Forgive me," she wrote, "Forgive me," she murmured, "Forgive me," she... blethered, shrieked, caterwauled. With a sigh I closed my notebook and returned it to the front pocket of my shoulder bag, consoling myself with the thought that Ernest Hemingway had written very little each day, sometimes going for weeks without a worthwhile sentence presenting itself. In tandem with this consoling thought came an image of a black and white photograph I'd seen in a biography of Hemingway; the author, white haired and white bearded, all rambunctious confidence gone, with the caption: "Hemingway's dazed and vacant stare reveals that the shock treatments at the Mayo Clinic may have damaged his memory. He has become a frail old man."

Decided against dwelling on Hemingway and instead turned to the back page of the *Evening Standard* to see what Tim Henman and his tennis cronies were up to, before attempting the crossword.

Aunty likes Tim Henman. She says he's quite nicely spoken for "that generation" and "at least he's got a full head of hair", which is a dig at my own favourite, Andre Agassi. She hates the Beckhams. Says, "The pair of them are just jumped up social climbers."

"Maybe, but they're very good looking."

"They're weird." After a minute adds, "Money can't buy breeding."

No longer allow myself to be drawn into her 'breeding' debate as this takes in her dislike of Wallace Simpson and the Abdication scandal, sometimes even bringing in the Hohenzollern chin.

I've realised that there are no toilets on this train. Tense-faced passengers tramping past, then back they come and set off in the other direction and back again, looking devastated as if they can't quite believe it. Hope I don't become tense-faced. Another hour to go. Shouldn't have drunk so much tea at Aunty's. Here comes another one – man in shorts. Serves him right. It is only March after all. He's asking for a cold in his Trossachs.

Something awful has just occurred. I have always had a problem with Adam's apples: Clint Eastwood's, Daniel Day Lewis's, to name but two. Now a man has sat down next to me who has an incredibly prominent Adam's apple and if that wasn't repulsively distracting enough, to one side of it (my side) is a large, red, pulsating pimple. It is truly horrible. I can almost feel the blood, nasty and infected, pumping away behind the protective layer of whatever the protective layer is made of. I am quelled. I am reduced in my seat. Yes, physically I've grown smaller. HE CAN'T SEEM TO LEAVE THIS PIMPLE ALONE! I want to tell him, "Men in your condition should be required by law to wear a polo neck or stay indoors."

Hang on, now he's wringing out his ear with his index finger. This is awful. For the first time in living memory I have no desire to break into my Kit Kat. Surely I'm not being neurotic. Put yourself in my position, sat next to a man who can't stop fiddling. To recap: once he'd made himself comfortable, i.e. accessed enough elbow room to attend to his pimple with ease, with his other hand he produced his mobile phone. Top of his voice telling someone, "I'm on the train," and much more about the time he intends to arrive, demonstrating a certain ignorance of rail travel.

Puts phone in trouser pocket, traces pimple thoughtfully before producing a Mars Bar. Doesn't he know people with pimples shouldn't be eating Mars Bars? Not only is this a sound medical fact but also, for the viewing public, a large weeping scarlet pimple in close conjunction with chocolate is a disgusting sight. And there you are, he manages to get chocolate on the inside thighs of his trousers, which is another disgusting sight. Ugh, chocolate-stained fingers return to pimple.

With some difficulty I whistle, "There's no business like show business," to disrupt his concentration, but no good. Suddenly he falls asleep, head back, mouth wide open and breathing loudly. The man opposite, trying to bury his face in his novel, winces visibly and we exchange furtive looks. The train pulls into Lewes and the weight of two commuters jiggling with their coats and bags wakes him.

But bloody hell, now the woman in the seat directly behind mine has just answered the call of the 1812 Overture. Took her three cannon shots before she found her mobile. She's talking at the top of her voice to someone called Pippa. Told Pippa and the rest of the carriage, "I'm almost at Glyn by the way." By the way of what? Now something's brilliant, fantastic and she's so pleased. Oh and Dad's been poorly but is on the mend.

Over to my left I can see another woman overdosing on Walkers crisps. She's put on a pair of sunglasses. It's ten to eight and pitch black outside! Hang on, crisp lady may have died. Her mouth's fallen open... but now it's closed again and she's started chewing. Uncle would have called that 'masticating'. 'Masticating' was one of his favourite dinnertime topics, telling us children that if we didn't masticate our food at least thirty times we'd have no teeth left by the time we were teenagers. (Pippa's being told about the computers being down at Brighton station and the screens were showing yellow and green bubbles instead of train times.) In retrospect I believe Uncle liked using the word 'masticating' in front of children. Why is it... (Emma and David say it's all fine in Dubai...) that mobile phone users, with the exception of my good self, do all the talking? This woman – not sunglasses and crisps, the 1812 – hasn't paused for breath. On the other end of the line, Pippa's probably trying desperately to get a word in edgeways.

Pippa: Actually I rang to say I've won the lottery and the tragic thing is I've only a week to live...

"So I said to Emma, I could do with a spell in Dubai myself the way the work's been piling up in the office."

Pippa: Only a day to live...

"I know what you mean, not enough hours in the day, minutes in the hour..."

Pippa: Aargh... Sound of body falling.

Which brings me almost up to date, although Uncle is gone but not quite forgotten and Aunty is unwillingly ensconced in a sheltered housing development.

I tell her, "Wish I lived here, Aunty, you're spoilt in the facilities department."

There's a communal conservatory, communal games room with a music centre, electric organ and a small kitchen off the games room for making snacks. Also a laundry and a rota which she refuses to adhere to and a guest bedroom which can be booked for that surprise guest. The place is like a women's commune, because no sooner do the men move down to the seaside than they sicken. First off, they imagine themselves sailor sorts, stand on the pebble beach searching the horizon and thinking of what might have been, then before the neighbours can say, "How's your father?", they've dropped dead of fatigue, discontent and broken hearts.

Aunty's establishment is run by a good and patient warden called Mrs Triffid. Of course this isn't her real name, it is an approximation hit on by Aunty. Sometimes she calls her "Mrs Tiffin", or "Mrs Titfer", which in Aunty parlance is a hat worn at a jaunty angle.

I arrived just after lunch and pressed the intercom button. Some moments later Aunty's voice crackled in my ear: "Is that you?"

"Yes it is."

"Push the door."

I push.

"Are you pushing?" she crackles.

"I'm pushing but it won't open."

But she's gone away. I press the button again.

"Did you push?" she crackles.

"Of course I pushed. It won't open."

"Push again."

I push. "Aunty, it won't open."

She's gone away.

I stopped pushing and shouting and set off along the side of the building. Behind me I heard her voice crackling from the intercom, "Are you in yet?"

I reached the side entrance and banged hard. Silence. Every single resident was either out or in a deep sleep. Stepped three paces back and bellowed up at her open window on the second floor, "Aunty, let me in."

Had visions of hundreds of aunties hobbling downstairs and along corridors to let in impatient nieces. At last through the glass doors I recognised a familiar figure in varying shades of lilac floral tottering down the communal staircase. She unlocked the door and let me in.

"Have you put on weight?"

"No," I replied tersely and leapt ahead of her up the stairs because she takes ages to pull herself up by holding onto both banisters. Outside her internal front door she's set an almost life-size straw donkey which she's bought from the Mencap charity shop. I know it's meant to be welcoming. In its back is a hollow for a cheerful pot plant but that day there was only a crumpled envelope marked "Milkman".

Inside her flat the central heating was on full blast, also random electric back-up radiators and the log-effect gas fire, which on consideration could not be a gas fire as it stood in the middle of the sitting room with a wire disappearing under the frayed rug.

"That heater is dangerous in the middle of the room. You could trip over the lead and set yourself and the whole building alight."

She came slowly through the front door, as if entering a completely alien environment, looking right and left, the expression on her face one of wonder. With her walking stick she poked the back of the settee and was reassured by it, seemingly fairly solid.

"Don't interfere," she said. "Did you get the boil-in-the-bag?"

This is so disgusting. Briefly, matey with the weeping pimple has just picked up somebody's discarded *Metro* magazine and turned to an article on Kim Basinger. There are several photographs of Kim wearing pretty revealing outfits. He's holding the magazine up to his face to better scrutinise Kim. It's as if he's trying to smell her. Then, horror of horrors, he starts pulling at his pimple... rhythmically. I think you appreciate what I'm implying here. For those with limited imagination, three syllables beginning with 'm' and not quite Uncle's old favourite 'masticate'. This is nightmarish. Would like to move down the carriage but carriage is very full and anyway I would have to negotiate his chocolate knees to get out into the gangway. Must shift my thoughts elsewhere. What is the woman with the Walkers crisps up to?

Aunty and I settled down amicably with a cup of tea apiece and a cream cake chosen from my bought cream cake selection. My tea plate was decorated with a Greek key pattern around the rim and a speckling of dried egg. I took off my glasses, so that the egg became invisible, and began on my very generously proportioned cream doughnut. Aunty sipped her tea daintily and held for the moment on choosing her cake.

"So how are you?" I shouted above televised highlights of the snooker, of which she is a great fan. Also a fan of tennis, darts, athletics and *Ready Steady Cook.*

"I've been better." She stuck out her bandaged leg. "The leg's pretty much as usual. It's my toenail that's been playing up."

"Really?"

"It's not just a run of the mill ingrown toenail."

"No?"

"Of course it's my own fault for trying to cut an oval shape. The nail's far too thick but I had to have a go."

"Did you?"

"Don't know how the devil I did it but as I levered the piece of nail growing into the flesh of my toe out with the nail scissors I went and stabbed myself. Took off a bloody great flap of skin." She made to roll down her elastic stocking.

"Don't!" I shouted. She looked up questioningly. "Not when I'm eating."

Looking most offended, she sat back against her crocheted cushions. However, by the time I'd finished my cake and reached for a second one, she'd forgotten all about her toenails and begun searching for her *Reader's Digest* Competition details.

Tum-tuddle tuddle tuddle tuddle – tum tum tum. Must say Pippa's a glutton for punishment. Hold this News Bulletin to report that the man wearing shorts and distressed expression is approaching passengers asking the whereabouts, if any, of lavatory. Has been advised to get off at Eastbourne and catch a later train. How much longer to Eastbourne? Only another half hour. Man looks excruciatingly distressed. My advice would be to make for the quiet of First Class and point his todger out of the sash window.

"Yes Pippa, I have got a Nectar card although Bill swears by Stanley Morgan. Bill says they're a discerning credit card company. They don't take all and sundry."

Oh god, I can't stand this much longer, the Scarlet Pimple is searching his pockets for something and if it's in his pocket it must be horrid. How many pockets can a pair of trousers have? Mum used to say I was too thin skinned by half, which makes me very thin skinned indeed. In Thomas Harris's *Hannibal,* Hannibal Lecter was able to remove his mind from the possibility of starved man-eating pigs eating his feet just by concentrating. Wish Hannibal Lecter was a real person with a book out on the subject. Seems trivial against his trials that I can't cope with pimple-scratching humanoid.

Ok, *Reader's Digest* Competition. Aunty waved a sheaf of colourful correspondence at me with a triumphant expression on her face.

"Aunty, it's all rubbish," I said dismissively. "You categorically won't win a prize."

She stared at me nonplussed, which is an old tactic as she's incapable of such a state.

"But I have already. They've sent me a box of chocolates and some kitchen knives. They're under your chair."

I put my plate down amongst the debris on the coffee table and pulled a cardboard carton from under my chair. Sure enough there was a box of Cadbury's Milk Tray and a set of six different Kitchen Devils. Also a book called *Country Walks of Great Britain,* plus an invoice for nineteen pounds, ninety-five pence, to include postage and packing. I looked at her. She looked defiantly back.

"You're welcome to inspect my details," she said, flourishing details like an elderly cheerleader. "I have to choose my preferred prizes, come the Grand Draw. I've gone for the twenty-six-inch plasma screen television rather than a month's holiday in Australia as subsidiary prize, and the fifty thousand pound second prize instead of the million pound first. That way they won't think I'm being greedy."

"I've told you, you will not win. They send this stuff out to thousands and thousands of people."

"It says, *Dear Mrs Storey*. It's a personal letter."

"No it isn't. It's a photocopy with your name inserted."

She lowered her bundle of letters into her lap. "It's only a bit of fun. I don't really expect to win."

She looked so dejected that I said reluctantly, "Well, you just might."

She brightened up immediately. "Do you think so?"

"Possibly, although I don't know anyone who has ever won."

Oh dear. Oh dear... now he's taken out some business papers and they're resting on his chocolate-stained knees. He's tweaking things out of his hair. What things can they be? Lice, grit, pustule shavings? Out with the phone: "Not long now. About another half hour, then let the party begin." And what kind of party would he be going to? A pimple-squeezing party? Man sitting opposite has had to cover his eyes with his hands. It's marginally worse for him. At least I'm only to one side. Regretfully, pimple side. Have buggered up my *Evening Standard* Friday Crossword which I look forward to doing every week. Have torn off a strip of the financial pages and am toying with the desire to write matey a note saying, LEAVE IT ALONE. YOU'RE MAKING ME FEEL SICK!

Across the gangway, the woman in sunglasses has taken down her bag from the luggage rack and produced a giant bag of Maltesers. Under normal circumstances would have found such behaviour unbearable: devouring several large packets of crisps and following up with Maltesers. The inside of her stomach must be in a sorry state. Who'd want to sit down to a plate of mashed crisps and Maltesers? However, next to my immediate neighbour, woman in sunglasses seems a decent, honourable woman, forced to eat unhealthy fare in lieu of usual pasta and green salad. Am tempted to offer her my Kit Kat but that would mean leaning across Red and Throbbing. Could imagine myself being overwhelmed by his fetid aura and fainting – possible mouth to mouth resuscitation by R & T would result in my suicide leap from moving train.

"Did I tell you about the plumber?"

"No." Took a large and satisfying bite of chocolate éclair.

"The waste disposal was blocked."

"Yes?" I said without interest. Don't know why they put waste disposals in residential units for the elderly. They're an accident waiting to happen.

"He told me he'd found half a finger down one, once."

"Please, Aunty. Not while I'm eating."

"For goodness sake, you young people are mighty squeamish. Anyway, he emptied it and it's working perfectly now."

"That's good." (Eclairs really are my favourite of all cakes although I perceive it's rather unfashionable to profess a liking for any sort of cake, bar those impregnated with muesli.)

"Astonishing what he pulled out. A great wad of hair and fat – looked like a boiled baby's head."

"Aunty! That's an appalling thing to say." I dropped the half-eaten éclair back onto my plate.

"You're such a sensitive soul." She was laughing cheerfully at me. "Pass the box, I'm ready for that cake now."

She chose the remaining éclair, held it up in front of her, looked thoughtfully. "You know, this reminds me of your uncle's..."

"I don't want to know."

Which makes me wonder how she would have dealt with this bloke. She'd certainly have noticed the pimple and his preoccupation with it. Probably saved the story up to put me off a future cream cake. She would have had no compunction about tapping him on his knee (no horror of coming into contact with chocolate stains). She'd have said something along the lines of, "Don't keep playing with it. Wait till you get in and then squeeze the bugger in front of the mirror. Nothing more satisfying. I envy you that pimple."

Eastbourne. Man in shorts, followed closely by similarly anxious-faced 1812 Overture, has hightailed it down the platform towards the toilets. Have a nasty feeling they may be locked at the weekend. And the best news is the Scarlet Pimple has also left the train. Hurrah! Man opposite has brought out his paperback – a Jeffrey Archer, but my mood is so improved I'll make no disparaging comment. Walkers crisps and sunglasses has finished eating and taken off her sunglasses. She has rather nice brown eyes. And I still have my Kit Kat, which I will unwrap luxuriously once the train gets going.

Putty

"Stroke her face," Aunty said, snuffling into a pink paper napkin retained from a visit to the Willow Cafe some weeks earlier.

"No way, Aunty. She looks as if she might bite."

"Just lay your hand on her ribcage then."

"Whatever for?"

"She's your mother. She'd be comforted to know you're here."

"She wouldn't. She'd be annoyed. Mum didn't welcome personal contact of the laying hands on her ribcage variety. You're her sister – you comfort her."

Aunty crushed the napkin against the buttons of her winter coat and stared fervently at a large gilt crucifix that hung, apparently unaided, from a velvet curtain.

"I can't do it. Oh Lord, take this burden from me." She shut her eyes tightly and said in a low monotone intended to give the slightly spooky impression that we might be at a séance, "The Lord is saying, *you* must do it."

"Why is the Lord telling you, not me?"

"I am the aunt and you the niece, the natural order is for the Lord to communicate through the senior person."

We were in an airless recess off the main chapel of rest. Most of the space was taken up by a large carved table bearing an open coffin. There were two chairs upholstered in red velvet for the mourners, red velvet effect carpet and encircling red velvet curtained walls. I imagined hell would be similarly furnished, only hotter.

I studied my aunt. Once upon a time she'd been a tall, shapely, strong-willed woman – not any more. She'd shrunk, grown frail – like a child, like a bird. A bird wearing a hand-knitted emerald green scarf and matching bobble hat.

"Come out of the way then," I said.

She sat down on one of the chairs, clutching her cloth shopping bag, while I edged past towards the coffin.

I considered myself an old hand with the dead, having buried several cats, one squirrel, and being the first person in Dad's hospital room only minutes after he'd died, the previous year. Dad had been sitting up in bed, very much in the position I'd left him in when I'd gone in search of sandwiches and a coffee.

"Don't like the look of their sandwiches," I'd said, making myself comfortable on a grey pre-formed plastic chair and resting my coffee cup on the windowsill. Only as I'd prepared to take a first bite of sandwich did I notice that dad was leaning slightly forward, away from the pillow and towards me – almost conversationally, as if he was about to impart a rather amusing insight into the workings of the National Health system as opposed to private care. I didn't touch him. I registered that same strange fear that he might suddenly snap his jaws at me.

"Dad?" I'd said, "Dad?"

But no, Dad was definitely elsewhere.

I hadn't expected Mum to feel as she did. Not so cold and hard, the cold permeating up through the unflattering brown and beige polyester silk dress she wore. She could have been carved from marble.

"Say goodbye," Aunty prompted.

"Goodbye Mum, from me and Aunty." I patted her ribs reassuringly.

"Is she breathing?" Aunty pulled her chair closer.

"She's dead. She's been embalmed... I expect."

"She was very beautiful."

Reluctantly I answered, "I'm sure she was, once."

"Everyone loved her."

Even with Mum lying dead in front of me, I couldn't allow that one to pass. "I don't know about everyone loving her. She was a very difficult, reserved woman."

"Don't speak ill of the dead. Your mother could light up a room. Men were putty in her hands."

"Not while I've been alive."

"Can't you even be pleasant about her now she's dead?" Aunty snapped.

Behind her, the curtains parted and the funeral director's disembodied head entered the room. "Everything ok?"

"Oh yes indeed, Mr Porter," Aunty gushed, as if Mum might be making a miraculous recovery under his ministrations.

"Good-oh. If you need me, I'm in reception." His head disappeared but there was no sound of him walking away.

"Has he gone?" she whispered.

I parted the curtains and peered out into an empty corridor. "No sign of him."

"I'm going to say a little prayer. It's what she would have wanted."

"Fair enough."

"You can say one too if you like."

"I'll just close my eyes."

I closed my eyes, hoping to daydream of my life resuming after Mum's funeral, after her affairs were finally settled. Instead Mum intruded. I saw her glass front door, the net curtain covering the glass in turmoil as if on the other side of it a violent fight was in progress. Finally the door opened several inches and Mum shot out onto the path kicking back at an unknown assailant. "Get in there, you devil," she shouted, slamming the door shut. Before she'd reached the gate, Mr Wu, her black and grey Pekingese dog, was up on the windowsill barking furiously.

"He nearly had me," she said.

"It's not as if he's an Alsatian, Mum, he's a tiny, sweet-natured dog."

"You try living with him then." Her voice softened and she turned and waved at him. I remember his eyes – dark and adoring.

"The nursing home should have put her in a long-sleeved dress," Aunty said suddenly, "Whatever were they thinking of? I don't believe that's even one of hers. I've never seen it before in my life."

I could hear her fidgeting – I opened my eyes. She'd taken off her emerald green scarf. "You'll have to help me shift her," she said.

"What?!"

"I want to get this scarf in and under her so that we can cover up her lower arms. All her age spots and whatever are on show – they look dreadful, as if she'd been a heroin addict."

"But Aunty, she's going to be cremated. Nobody else will see Mum's arms."

"I don't care."

"Can't you just drape the scarf across her?"

"No. That would look football hooliganish. Now, if we loop the scarf so that it flows across her arms as if it was a stole and she was off to a party…"

"We shouldn't tamper," I said desperately, but Aunty was already on her feet and poking around in the satin lining of the coffin.

"Shouldn't we get Mr Porter?"

"No, we'll manage between us. Oh come on, you're a strapping young woman. Take her shoulders."

Gingerly I took Mum's shoulders and lifted.

"Mind her head, it's drooping backwards," Aunty said as she fed the scarf under Mum's body.

"Hurry up, Aunty. Oh this is horrible. Mum's eyes are opening."

"They can't be. They stitch them down."

"I can see the whites of her eyes – I'll have to lower her."

"If you lower her now, my hands will be trapped underneath. Use your elbows to support her head."

I used my elbows. Mum's half-open eyes closed again. Aunty pulled the scarf up between Mum's arm and the far side of the coffin.

"Lower away. Now doesn't that look better?" Aunty was quite rejuvenated. She peered into Mum's face. "If only they'd left in her teeth, she'd still have her lips."

Together we stood looking down into the coffin. I remembered Mum sitting at her messy dressing table, making up her face as if it was a canvas. My skinny, unmaternal mother outlining her lips with a scrappy lip brush, then filling in the shape she'd made with orangey lipstick. A tissue to blot away any excess and she'd sit back to consider her reflection in the mirror with great satisfaction.

"Not bad," she'd say, "not bad at all."

"We could do her lips," I said.

Aunty shot me a quick, hopeful look. "Could we? Not much to work on – her top lip's disappeared completely."

"I'll draw it back in."

Using Aunty's Tangerine Pink, I made Mum's harsh line of a mouth smile. I put colour back in the cheeks that a fifty-cigarettes-a-day habit had obliterated. I drew in her Joan Crawford eyebrows. Here was my mother asleep, dreaming of something that lightened her dissatisfied spirit.

"Perhaps comb her hair forward?" Aunty suggested.

"No, that's enough."

"I'll say when it's enough."

"We've still got to choose the flowers."

"Roses. She was like a rose."

"She was not."

"They were her favourite flower."

"No, they weren't. If she liked any flower it was nicotiana."

I held aside the curtain for Aunty to pass through. We both hesitated. In my head I was thinking, "That's it, then."

Wiping her eyes, Aunty said, "Dot didn't have much time for tears."

Which jolted me. My mum changed back to Dot, changed back to Auntie's younger sister. A beautiful, beloved Dot, turning men to putty.

"Mr Wu's heartbroken," Aunty said, "He'll never get over this."

"Yes, I expect you're right," I said, and I let the curtain drop.

Like Sisters

"He was a working dog," she told me, "Not a runt but timid. There were four other dogs at the farm. They ganged up on him, day in, day out. I believe we saved Him's life."

That's what she calls the dog, Him. I often see them up on the West Hill when I'm walking across to visit Karen. It's a proper grassy hill running down towards the Old Town and the sea. A place where people walk their dogs and on windy afternoons fly kites. It's been three years since I brought Karen up here. It used to be her favourite place. We'd sit and eat our sandwiches on one of the benches. Strange to think it was always Karen, not me, who made the sandwiches and flask of hot chocolate. She couldn't do that now.

Him is frightened of almost everything: other dogs, extreme weather, children, traffic. He freezes, lies down on his belly with his paws stretched out like a collie watching over sheep. Him's eyes are shut though. He doesn't want to see whatever's going on. It can take anything between five minutes and an hour before he'll feel secure enough to start walking again.

I don't know what the young woman's name is. I can see she's used to talking to strangers, she talks without appearing to monitor her words. Today she said, "I love Him more than the bloke I live with, and I love him a lot."

"Does your bloke love Him too? They're not jealous of each other?"

She shook her head.

It started to rain. I decided not to put up my red umbrella. She knelt on the wet grass beside Him, pulling gently on his worn leather lead.

"We can't stay out all afternoon," she said, stroking the dog's head.

"He doesn't want to budge," I said, stating the obvious for something to say. She looked up and smiled. I don't think she recognised me although I'd spoken to her on several similar occasions. I held my hand near his muzzle.

"Better not. If he doesn't know your smell, he could nip you."

She rolled the dog onto his back. He looked like any other playful collie cross-breed, waving his rangy black and white legs in the air. Only, his eyes remained closed. She rubbed his stomach. "It's all right," she said.

I liked her face. It was coloured pink with a translucent light tan as if she spent a lot of time outside – which, obviously, she does. She has a squint which makes her face interesting rather than pretty. It's as if she's able to focus intently on just one thing.

I told her, "I'm off to see my friend, Karen. She's very ill. We've known each other for years. We're more like sisters than friends."

"Are you?" she said, but with no genuine interest in her voice. I envied her that dog. I envied the dog. Eventually they would get to their feet and walk away. Even if they stayed where they were, neither really seemed to mind.

The rain came down harder.

"You're both going to get wet."

"It was three months before he came out from under the kitchen table," she said.

"Then he's doing very well now."

I didn't like my voice. Its tone was too bright and encouraging. They didn't need any encouragement from me.

"Well, goodbye," I said.

"Bye. I hope your friend gets better soon." She smiled but I didn't get a true sense that she actually saw me. She'd rolled Him onto his stomach again and begun scratching his chin.

I walked on. It was absolutely necessary for me to do all the things I always did for Karen: change, wash, feed her, as if she were a small child. But she would never know me, not any more. My voice would not soothe her. She would not recognise, from any smell or touch of mine, that I had once been her lover.

I kept wanting to tell someone – now that it was too late. Karen was lost. The life we'd shared was lost. There was nobody who could verify our love. "Dear friends," we'd said about ourselves, "Like sisters."

At the top of the steps taking me down to Wallinger's Walk, I looked back. What I hoped to see was the two of them heading away into the sheeting rain. She would glance back over her shoulder and see me watching, possibly raise her hand. I would raise my red umbrella. It would be a cheerful moment at odds with the weather. But no, the woman and her dog hadn't moved. She was still hunkered down, one hand on Him's back, squinting out towards the sea.

Swallowtail

Con wedged the dog's head between the palms of his hands and kissed its muzzle. "Wake me at eight. All right, Jimmy Boy?"

The whites of its eyes showed and one ear twitched as a door closed somewhere downstairs. Jimmy Boy watched Con settle on the narrow bed, a navy jumper tucked around his feet, an old shawl of his gran's over his shoulders. The bed springs creaked as Con tightened into a ball. From beneath a fold of crochet, Con peered out at the dog. "Coming up to keep me warm then?"

The dog didn't move.

"Fuck you then," Con said quite cheerfully as he closed his eyes.

Jimmy Boy pattered across the room, curled into a corner and slept.

A mile away on the third storey of a five-storey block in Stamford Hill, Marty oiled his smooth, shaved legs. He liked his legs. He liked the oil and the sun and the close, town-smelling fresh air. He frowned when in a nearby garden a child started crying, the intensity of its sorrow unsettling his good mood for a moment.

There wasn't room to lie out on his two metres of balcony,

so he sat on a flowered canvas chair, the soles of his bare feet flat against the railings. His legs were a rich brown from afternoons in the park. Nervy afternoons in tight shorts that showed the vulnerable curves of his buttocks, a crisp white singlet, gold chains around his throat and wrists. Marty was cautious, fearful of derision, a smack in the mouth and worse, yet he was still proud of his body – sensitive to the odd interested glance that turned to disappointment when it reached his lined face and thinning white-blonde hair. Nowadays, that happened often, the whispered exchanges, sniggers of the young and confident. While hating the young, theirs was the interest he craved.

On his left shoulder was a small tattoo. A cartoon butterfly, crude red and green etched with indigo. He'd taken a drawing with him to the tattooist of a male swallowtail: yellow and black with red and blue false eyes. The tattooist barely glanced at it. He did his own thing – badly – but his butterfly served its purpose: the bright colours drew the eye to the perfect skin of Marty's shoulders and neck.

At five o'clock Marty went inside for his bath. Afterwards, still in his dressing gown, he ate ham and mustard sandwiches and sipped a cup of unsweetened tea. He stood at the balcony door looking out; soon the sun would dip behind the flats opposite. It was September, another summer almost over.

He cleaned his teeth, then dressed. He drank whisky and water – two tumblers. Marty would have preferred the whisky neat but whisky neat was for bad times when day repeated day and he felt he was neither at the centre nor even the edge of what could be called a life. Some evenings in the pub, Dennis the barman would shift him out of the way, maroon him at a side table facing gangrenous plants that blocked any street light from shining through the windows.

"For your own safety," Dennis said, hand firm on Marty's shoulder. "I have to consider the customers, Marty. And no hanky-panky. You know what I mean."

Dennis's customers didn't like Marty. They didn't like the way he stroked his wrists and forearms as if his own touch gave him pleasure, his low insidious murmurings, limpid eyes searching the crowded room for recognition, just a flicker of interest. Even hostility meant an awareness had been achieved; some pressure point within someone activated; for a brief moment he was the object of attention.

This particular Sunday evening, jazz engulfed the pub, drowning speech, cancelling out movement. This evening, Con and Jimmy Boy came to Marty's table.

Con came in every Sunday without fail but he'd never sat down with Marty before. He always trailed way behind Jimmy Boy, some nights several paces behind, others several minutes; pale, thin and hesitant. It was a standing joke amongst the regulars. Not a cruel one. They liked the stoicism of the dog and felt sorry for Con. He seemed too young to be nourished on alcohol and cigarettes.

Marty didn't want Con at his table. He had no use for him. He recognised that Con lived in a world of his own which didn't even come close to his. Also Con was in his early twenties and Marty wanted no adverse comparisons made. That night he was concentrating on a man at the bar wearing a dark red shirt and black trousers. He could see him through the crowd of twisting, turning bodies, through the music, the smoke, voices. One evening, perhaps that evening, he might come to Marty's table. He just might. It had happened in the past.

The tired flesh of Marty's face felt rosy and firm; blood pulsed excitedly below its surface. His lips reddened and gleamed wetly beneath his neat, greying moustache. The standing-room-only ten o'clock crowd pressed at his back. At Con's back. The grizzled dog cramped himself smaller beneath the table. Marty felt his attention slipping and the thread between himself and the man at the bar grow slack. The man had gone.

"You shouldn't bring a dog in here," he said to Con.

"He brings me."

Con didn't look up. With a spent match, he continued to trace patterns in the spilt beer and ash on the table. He had long fingers, smooth blue-grey skin. Nails were nicotined ovals rimmed neatly with black. Fascinated, Marty stared at them before looking down at his own hands, hidden in his lap, nails shiny with pink varnish.

Another drink and Con's presence ceased to annoy him. Con was hardly noticeable, retreating into a blur of spinning images. Marty saw only himself, the self he loved and was true to. He rested his arm on the table. Pushing back his shirtsleeve, almost reverently he began to stroke his skin, admiring the warm peach of his inner arm, its texture; almost a woman's arm.

"You've beautiful skin." Con's soft voice – yet Con's head was still bent over his delicate world of alcohol patterns.

"Did you say something?" Marty asked.

Con's heavy, white lids lifted. His blonde hair fell back from his white-boned forehead. He offered Marty a slack, open-mouthed smile.

"What did you say?" Marty asked again.

"You've beautiful skin." Con pushed a half-empty packet of cigarettes towards Marty. "I've been watching you for weeks and tonight I thought I might say something."

He took up another match and began to draw again.

With difficulty Marty focused on Con's drooping head, the flutter of dark lashes. It was the first time in many years he'd felt warmth for himself coming from someone else. He'd ceased to hope, finally forgotten hope had ever existed.

Con touched his arm, drawing him back. "Take me home with you."

The words lay gently between them. With shaking hands, Marty gathered his cigarettes, his lighter, took a last drink, leaving his glass one third full.

Jimmy Boy had moved and was lying on the rough matting in the doorway, waiting patiently. Con rose unsteadily to his feet and they both followed Marty out into the night. The early evening warmth had disappeared, rain spattered their faces, cleared their heads – woke them up.

Marty closed the window and wiped rain from the sill with a tea towel before drawing the faded orange curtains. He switched on the standard lamp, the bedside lamp, switched off the overhead light. Con sat silently at the table. He seemed at ease, his eyes following Marty. Marty, nervous, fumbled in a low cupboard for glasses and whisky, unpleasantly aware of his thinning hair as he bent forward. He straightened to find Con smiling, the warmth between them from the pub persisting.

He poured their drinks. Poured water into a soup bowl for Jimmy Boy and laid it humbly on the plastic mat in front of the sink, willing the creature to like him, Con to say, *He doesn't take to many people.* The dog sniffed then refused the water, sinking down at Con's feet, head on his paws, eyes twitching rapidly behind closed lids.

"You don't have to do anything," Marty said, touching Con's hand. He half expected Con to flinch away. "I'd like you to watch, that's all. If it's too embarrassing, tell me. I'll stop. No problem. I won't be offended. I'd rather you said."

He gulped his drink, waiting for a word or a sign to proceed.

"Whatever."

The word shivered in front of him. When he closed his eyes it remained in dancing red letters. He began to arrange the room, positioning a tall mirror at the side of the bed, tilting the shade of the bedside lamp. Over the top section of the mirror he hung a pale green towel. From a small suitcase in his wardrobe he brought a deep-purple, woman's dressing gown, edged with a band of black lace. He draped it, skirt spread out, on the bed. Lovingly he stroked the cloth.

Finally, Marty sat down within the skirt of the dressing gown and facing the mirror. He pulled the cloth around him, up and over the waistband of his trousers, till his hips and thighs were covered. He sat quite still, staring at his reflection. His head in the mirror image was obliterated by the green towel. He saw a lover and a loved one's body. His hands were the hands of the lover as they unbuttoned his shirt and caressed the creamy skin beneath. Loving hands drew on the dressing gown, cupped his small fleshy breasts, pressing them close, the lamplight deepening the shadow between them. Gracefully he slid his arms into the silken sleeves of the robe and knotted the sash tight at his waist. Marty's fingers trailed along the column of his neck and across his collar bone. He was mesmerised by the vibrant mirrored image.

"Let me be your mirror," Con said.

Con's hands, light and tentative, stroked Marty's body. Down over his breasts, Con's fingers circling Marty's nipples, then across his belly. He knelt in front of Marty, opening his flies, easing Marty's trousers over his hips.

"No," Marty whispered.

Con pressed his lips to Marty's silken thighs.

"Yes," Con said, taking Marty's penis into his mouth.

"No," Marty said again, but he held Con's head against him as his hips strained against Con's young, hot mouth.

Con lay sleeping, his body forming a foetal position, hands and wrists between his thighs. Marty next to him was wakeful, weaving tenuous dreams for their future. After about an hour, he felt Con's body tense as he raised himself jerkily onto one elbow and stared blankly around the room. Jimmy Boy sat yawning, eyes fixed on Con. Con's body relaxed.

"Time to go," he said, half to Jimmy Boy.

"Stay. It's almost dawn. I'll make breakfast."

"No. I've got to go. I'll see you again."

Con was already up, pulling on his clothes and making for the door.

"But when? Surely you needn't go straight away. Have another drink, a coffee. It was all right, wasn't it?"

He felt foolish and vulnerable as his words spluttered out, just an aging old queer in a gaudy dressing gown, pleading for a few more minutes.

"You'll see me again. I'm going nowhere."

Con paused at the door. Behind him, Marty fussed, his hands fluttering at Con's jacket.

"I can return the favour. I can do most things. Or nothing. I'm trying to say I'm flexible."

Con turned and smiled. He kissed Marty on the corner of his mouth, intimately. "See you, mate."

*

Marty didn't think he'd be able to sleep. Instead he tidied away the glasses and bottle, straightened his bed, all the while talking to himself.

"Nothing's that easy. Chalk and cheese. Don't, don't, don't build your hopes." To his reflection he said, as he manhandled the mirror back into its usual place, "You're a silly sod, Marty."

He ran hot water into the sink and began to rinse the glasses. It was only then he noticed the bowl he'd put down for Jimmy Boy, empty. He knelt on the floor, patting around the plastic mat to see if the bowl had tipped over, but no, mat and bowl were bone dry.

THE MARINE VIEW CHRONICLES

1

Shirley Poppy

It's three o'clock on a wet, miserable, January afternoon. It seems darker here at three than it did yesterday in Burgess Hill. Not a sound – funereal, punctuated by a lavatory being flushed every five minutes or so somewhere on the floor below. Robert and Jackie have gone back to London. They had to get off early to avoid driving through the city in the rush-hour. They explained this carefully as if the rush-hour hadn't been part of my routine for nearly forty years. I'm a job well done. Mother, sealed, Sellotaped and sent off on an eternal holiday to the seaside.

"A home, residential, Mother. Almost a hotel. Almost home from home."

Like bloody hell it is.

"We can't have you getting ill again."

I'm old enough and ugly enough to look after myself – only I wasn't, not any more.

Old age, they're both scared it will catch up with them. Even now, it's too damn close for comfort. So here I sit – hunched woman in bright green dress. My eyes say it all. I'm terrified and the only thing between myself and that fear is blind, impotent rage.

I'd thought we understood one another. Robert – my friend, my son. Always, "What's cooking Mum – my mum – best mum – best girl."

One hour ago, standing in the doorway of this room.

"You'll be fine here, Mum, the owner's a really nice woman."

Jackie downstairs in the hall: "Robert, are you coming?"

He even had tears in his eyes. "We'll see you soon."

What will 'soon', be? Four to six weeks?

"Can't get away, we're working, Mum."

Birthday, Christmas?

"We both need this holiday."

Easter, bank holidays?

"Did you get our flowers?"

I'm to be a guest with five other ladies. A Jean Matthews will take good care of me, and it will no doubt all be a laugh a minute.

Several weeks have passed, seems at least six months. The house? Large. On the sea front, although you can't actually see the sea front unless you're in one of the upper rooms because of the high laurel hedge running three sides of the front garden. There's a garden at the back as well, with a lawn and blue hydrangeas – my least favourite shrub, but no trouble, you see. Ditto the white plastic urns on patio and porch. Easy to shift and keep clean. Fill 'em up – daffodils and wallflowers, all change to fuchsia and geraniums come summer. I can hardly wait to see what Jean's got up her sleeve for winter and autumn. Inside, the walls are painted orange or mustard

– satin finish emulsion. Wipe-clean warmth and cheerfulness. Not so the bathrooms and toilets – gun-metal grey walls and maroon lino; towels, thin and worn as old tea cloths.

I've made no real friends amongst my fellow residents – it's too late in the day for me to want to make the required effort. Now and again, I'm still able to take a little walk. I prefer my own company to that of comparative strangers.

And what of Jean Matthews? Well, so far, I like her very much. Everyone here likes Jean.

Odd to think, she is only about fifteen years my junior, in her early sixties. There's a youthful, eager quality about her I find endearing. She wears white tee-shirts and navy trousers; something crisp and nautical about her, and as strong and muscular as a man. I sense she's at ease with her body. My son would squirm if I said that to him: Jean Matthews is at ease with her body.

"Don't be smutty, Mother – it isn't like you."

She looks after us well. I don't envy her the job. She is a galvaniser; we, her inadequate troops, shuffling off at tangents instead of marching briskly to do her bidding.

Then there is Whiz, real name Elizabeth, who helps out during the week. She is thirty, she seems much younger. Very pretty – sillyish, I think, but pleasant enough.

And how am I? Who am I? Am I coping? How do I look?

I look my age and a little more, seventy-nine. Not too lined of face, instead I have folds and shadows. Fortunately, I've never been pretty. I was considered handsome, an impressive woman. I improved with the years, until a certain age and then it was downhill all the way.

When I was born, I had thick red baby hair. Christened Shirley after the Shirley Poppies flowering for a day in my grandmother's garden. As I grew up, I secretly saw myself as a strong and graceful plant, always wore green. Where do they go, those younger selves with shining hair and smooth faces? We step so lightly into the tunnel, emerge years later, eyes weak against the sun, steps heavy – we are old.

Robert and Jackie think I'm becoming senile because I don't talk any more. Not true – I choose not to talk. I can't bear the sound of my voice; the words that choose to spill out of my mouth – all fused into one long wail of dissatisfaction.

It surprises me. It wasn't to be expected but sometimes I find myself enjoying being here. My evenings are spent in the kitchen with Jean and Whiz, except Saturdays and Sundays, when Whiz goes home to her parents' house.

The two of them draw me out. I can't think why I should have been chosen above my other colourless sisters, but whatever purpose my presence serves for them, I believe they're fond of me. Whiz still seems like a child, but I can't help myself. I've given in – she makes me laugh even if it's only inside – she's so damn daft.

It's her eyes and voice. There's a joyful quality – hard to explain, normally I'd be cynical of 'joyful', be thinking, what's she got to be joyful about, silly madam? She's quite tall with long brown hair tied back from her face with a ribbon. I find myself thinking, which is ridiculous, "She and Jean are made for each other." Except they're both women and there's the boyfriend, Paul Bradley.

Jean calls him Mr Bradley, enquiring solemnly after his health. It's Jean's little joke. It amuses us.

"And how is Mr Bradley keeping?"

"Mr Bradley's more than fine, thank you, Jean."

"More than fine, eh? Must be very fine indeed. Will there be wedding bells and a bridal gown, come spring?"

"I bloody well hope not."

Jean's always teasing Whiz – Whiz doesn't seem to mind at all.

Like the rest of the house, the kitchen is old-fashioned in a welcoming way. No modern worktops and cupboards; wooden cabinets painted cream with etched glass doors. In the middle of the room is a red Formica table with four matching chairs, red quarry tiles on the floor. Busy Lizzies and fuchsia in different coloured plastic pots on the windowsill. Always a cutting of something or the other in a jam jar, the water going cheerfully stagnant. In the corner of the room there's an old boiler that Jean keeps lit all year round for the hot water, an open packet of Zip fire lighters and a pair of sooty orange gloves leaning against the black pipe that runs through to the outside wall. Comfortable on cushions in my cane chair brought in from the sitting room, cigarettes and matches, a red tin ashtray balanced on my knees, I come alive.

Jean has an oil lamp she bought in the 1960s that she cleans and tends at least once a week. The table gets littered with twists of newspaper, razor blades, dusters, polish, as she carefully trims the pale grey wick, hair falling thick and a grizzled white over her forehead. The kitchen smells of paraffin and whatever we've had for dinner that evening. Whiz sits the other side of the table – I can't always read her expression. I hear her voice and know she's contented.

Suddenly, I need to see my body in its entirety. I want to know just how bad it is. I've no full-length mirror, no privacy anyway. There are no locks on the doors, even – especially – the bathroom door. My self-inspection is hasty and furtive.

At any moment the door could open, yet Jean wonders why I don't want to wash or bathe more often.

"No one will come in without knocking."

"But Jean, that implies someone will knock and come in."

"Would they want to look at you?"

"Well, thank you very much, but that's hardly my point."

In the mirror of the bathroom cupboard I can see my bony shoulders and mad, toothpaste smile. I look down between my long breasts, my belly glows pale and furrowed, my feet clench into the bathmat like two tight red fists... Footsteps on the landing outside and I pull my dressing gown on again.

Regarding the 'to wash or not to wash' debate. For just so long I get away with a lick and a promise in the morning, nothing at night, then Jean swoops, like a hawk onto an angry, hostile squirrel: "Shirley, bath seven o'clock. Bring a fresh nightdress, you've had that pink one on for over a fortnight."

She washes me as if I'm a six-year-old orphan that, by god, she'll do her duty by – firm hand in a rough flannel, dealing with my face and body, scolding as she works.

"Getting to be a bad habit. I don't like it. We're residential, not nursing. If you can't manage...

"I can manage."

"Why don't you then?"

"I've told you..."

"And I've told you."

She's relentless, knocks retorts out of me like feathers from a pillow. It's what we need, whether we like it or not. She keeps us up to scratch. We know she cares about us: tough as she is, she can't stop the odd soft note creeping into her voice; and afterwards, when I'm dry and powdered and sitting up in bed, the pair of us are pleased. I quite like the rosy-faced lady with the clean peppery hair I see in my silver hand mirror. She leaves me with a clutch of magazines and later brings up a cup of sugary Horlicks.

It's been months now. It's summer. I find I look forward to small things: what's for afternoon tea, another sunny day, will our communal moggy pick my room for its daily siesta? There's no halfway house with me. It's either/or, and the more I become a part, the less I think of Robert – and Jackie hardly enters my mind at all. I remember them – sometimes with difficulty.

They send their love and I send mine back – it counts for little. They take me for an airing, we begin and end the day as the strangers we've become. They're no longer relevant to my life. They've cramped me into this small world and I'm greedy for the little available. Here, some live for food, others for the television. Me? I live for Jean and Whiz and my cigarettes.

"Rub my back, Jean, I can't sleep."

"We spoil you."

"That's better. You should have been a masseur."

"I should have been a lot of things."

The heels of her hands pummelled my shoulder blades, then the top of my spine. She poured a few drops of lavender oil into the palms of her hands and smoothed it over my neck, rubbing it gently into the follicles of my hair at the base of my skull. I didn't feel soothed, I was wide awake thinking: "If I was naked instead of lost in an old woman's nightdress, if my breasts were still creamy with delicate blue veins; if I were even twenty years younger, instead of fifteen years older. If, if, if only..."

"That's your lot."

Her weight shifted from the side of the bed. I didn't

want her to go, I said quickly, "Robert and Jackie thought a watercolour for that wall."

"Oh yes?" She edged towards the door.

"What do you think, watercolour or oil?"

"Couldn't say. You've got to live with it."

"But if the choice was yours."

"It isn't mine. Try and get some sleep."

"I'm not sleepy."

"Well, I am. I've been up since six."

"Am I very selfish?"

"Very. I'll see you in the morning."

"You're not annoyed, are you, Jean?"

"Just weary, now night-night."

I listened to her fading steps on the stairs, heard her lock and bolt the front door. It was ten past one. I switched off the bedside lamp. The second hand of the clock ticked louder in the silence, like a mouse chattering in a cupboard.

Whiz always brought up my tea at eight o'clock sharp. The following morning she came in half an hour late. She looked tired and ill-humoured.

"Tied one on with Mr Bradley?" I asked cheerfully.

"Call him Paul, for goodness sake, that's Jean's silliness."

She helped me into a sitting position against the pillows, sniffed the air disapprovingly.

"Why don't you let me get you something flowery from Boots? That lavender oil of yours smells disgusting."

"I like it. It reminds me of my childhood."

"You've had that bottle for ages, doesn't it ever run out?"

"When it does, I'll buy some more."

"You will not."

She went across to the window and attacked the curtains.

"You're not in a very good mood this morning."

"I'm irritated."

"With me?"

"Don't be silly, with bloody Jean."

"Now, Whiz."

"She gets on my nerves. 'Mr Bradley this, Mr Bradley that,' it's not funny any more."

"I expect she's a little jealous."

The words slipped out. I didn't mean them until I'd said them. Whiz froze, then her shoulders loosened, and she pressed her face forward against the window pane.

"I expect she is," she said quietly.

It was my first birthday in the Home – I was due a celebratory outing. Robert and Jackie would take me first for lunch, then a drive, then to tea. I was to be washed, groomed and put through my paces as if they'd entered me for Crufts.

"Make an effort, Shirley," Jean said the day before. "You can talk when you want to. In the kitchen you chatter away nineteen to the dozen."

That evening she gave me a bath and let me come down again to the kitchen for two birthday sherries. I felt truly special, fussed over. My glass of sherry glinted like gold; a new packet of twenty cigarettes from Jean perched next to it on top of the boiler. Whiz had bought me a lilac shawl and I wore it, falling prettily (or so I imagined) around my shoulders. I'm not fond of shawls but lilac was a colour that suited me.

Jean sat down at the table and drew the oil lamp to her.

"Now, birthday girl, have you heard the latest?"

"See no evil, hear no evil, speak no evil, that's me these days," I said. I was becoming quite a wit. Jean applied Brasso to the base of the lamp, then paused to look at me, her eyes twinkling.

"Our Mr Bradley's been lying in the middle of the road to prove his undying love. Had a near miss last night with a Land Rover."

"Don't spoil the evening," Whiz said sharply from her position by the sink.

"In her very words," Jean nodded towards Whiz, "he's a scream, quite mad, likes a bit of fun."

"But what if he gets run over?" I asked.

"Not our Mr Bradley, apparently he's very nimble."

"Leave it alone, Jean."

"Well, as long as he's nimble," I said.

"Exactly. As long as Mr Bradley stays nimble, doesn't get old and decrepit." There was an edge to her voice. Her eyes no longer looked at me, nor were they twinkling. Whiz splashed water into the washing-up bowl.

"Cup of tea, Shirley?" Whiz asked.

"Shirley's still on sherry," Jean said. "Can we get back to Mr Bradley and what he'll do for love?"

"It's none of your business."

"It is my business. You know it's my business. You've made it my business." Jean threw down the duster and put her head in her hands. Nobody spoke. Then Whiz came and stood next to her, gently stroking the back of Jean's neck.

"Please don't keep on, Jean," she said, her voice soft.

"I'm sorry."

"Whatever will Shirley think?"

"Shirley thinks nothing," I shouted from my chair.

"Sorry, sorry, sorry," Jean said.

Whiz pulled her hair. "You're a silly sod," she said, and bent and kissed the top of Jean's head.

*

Sunday, my birthday. Outing day, the day we're ferried from tea shop to stately home, in that order of importance, by friends and relatives. Those left behind go for a drive in the minibus driven by Lily from the Salvation Army, leaving Jean in the kitchen, preparing her 'welcome home' Sunday supper, which is about the same as any other day of the week but with cream cake.

I waited in my room wearing a dress of green and black silk, grey stockings and uncomfortable black patent shoes with a small heel. I clutched my leather handbag against my stomach. In it were my cigarettes, matches, a hanky and my lipstick – an orangey shade I'd had for years. I'd hooked my walking stick over the back of my chair and my raincoat was freshly pressed, hanging on the back of the door. They never arrived when they said they would. Sometimes I spent an hour listening for the sound of their car. My face became stiff waiting to give birth to its welcoming smile.

Along the landing, I heard Stella come out of her room and knock for Doris. Hilda made her fourth visit to the toilet, then I could hear them all assembled down in the hall and Lily's voice ringing out above their birdlike twittering, "Have you all been?"

"YES," came the chorus and the sound of laughter.

Jean knocked on my door and came in.

"Come on, birthday girl, give your kids a surprise. Meet them down in the hall for a change."

So I was shunted from bedroom chair to hall chair. I sat staring at the oak front door, wishing I still had the power in my legs to run.

After lunch, they finally stopped talking about themselves. Robert was driving slowly – already they were both searching out a place to stop for tea.

"Present giving goes with tea and cakes," Jackie said.

"So Mum, what have you been up to?"

"Nothing much."

"Been out on the sea front?"

"No."

"Sat in the garden?"

"No, Robert."

"What have you done then?"

"I told you, nothing."

"But you must do something all day," Jackie said brightly. "Oh Robert, look at that garden. Isn't it fabulous? What would I give for a display like that?"

He pulled the car into the kerb. "Look at that, Mum, you used to like gardening."

I looked – said nothing. Salvias, dahlias, geraniums, gladioli, poppies – hot reds shimmering in the sunshine.

"Mum, are you paying attention?" Robert sounded irritated.

"Yes."

"Well, what do you reckon, then?"

"She's not interested, Robert."

"She should be interested. What do you think of that garden, Mum?"

"I don't like red."

They looked at each other, completely bewildered. His Adam's apple moved under his shirt collar.

"Mother, I can see green grass, pink, orange, white and blue flowers. There's poppies too. You've always liked poppies."

"I don't like red," I said again. "I used to. I don't any more."

"Fine." He twisted the ignition sharply. "We'll take you back now. You don't like red, you don't like anything, so we won't waste any more of our time."

"Robert, there's no point getting angry. She doesn't understand." Jackie leaned across the gears and patted his thigh.

"Oh she understands all right, don't you, Mother?" He caught my eye in the driving mirror. "You bloody understand."

We swerved into the drive. Jackie tried to help me out, but I was having none of it. I didn't dawdle; I grabbed my stick and walked as fast as I'm capable, back inside. Behind me, I heard Robert shouting: "Get her raincoat and handbag, Jackie. Where's that damn present?"

It was cool in the hall, smelt of the pine cones Jean collected in autumn and left in old chipped bowls on every windowsill. I knew the smell of the house now and liked it. I made for the kitchen and Jean with her Sunday paper, the surety of a strong cup of tea and my own familiar chair.

I thought I barged in noisily. If I did, they didn't hear me. How foolish they were in any case – in front of the kitchen window in broad daylight, but then perhaps I'm the fool to imagine that would matter to them. I didn't understand at first. I thought Jean was comforting Whiz, or Whiz was comforting Jean, and then I saw that Whiz's blouse was undone, her white brassiere pulled down on one side, so that her breast was exposed and Jean's hand was cupping it, as if holding something precious.

"Mum, the present. Good god, whatever's going on?" Robert pushed past me into the room. Whiz turned away towards the window; Jean faced us as if ready to die rather than let us hurt her.

"Do you mind?" she said. "This is my kitchen."

I shoved Robert out into the hall and closed the door.

"Robert, your mother's things, you could have helped," Jackie complained from the hallway. The house seemed full of their noise and movement. It needed quiet – to slip back into normality.

"Just leave everything and go," I said.

"Now look here, Mother..."

"No more talk, I've had enough..."

"You've had enough. That's priceless."

"Robert, calm down."

"Do you know the pretty scene my mother has just been subjected to?"

"It doesn't matter," I said.

"I'll bloody decide whether it matters or not."

"For heaven's sake, haven't we had enough unpleasantness this afternoon?" Jackie dropped my coat and bag onto the stairs and leant the promised watercolour next to them. They both started shouting at each other. I thought of Jean and Whiz in the kitchen listening.

"They'll have to come out of the kitchen eventually and when they do..."

"I'm sick and tired of this, Robert. I'll wait for you in the car." Exit Jackie.

Robert was punching the palm of one hand with the fist of the other. My fingers closed around both his hands and drew them together, stilling them.

"Don't worry, Mum, I'll sort this out."

"You'll mind your own business." My fingers tightened. I have a good grip – no rheumatism. Surprising strength for such an old lady. He was surprised. I was starting to hurt him.

"Let go, Mum."

Robert has such smooth, well-kept hands. I pressed my thumbnails into the soft flesh.

"Mum, you're hurting me."

He tried to shake me off. You'd think that would be easy – a well-built, healthy man shaking off a fleshless body of almost eighty. It's the bond between mother and son – always there – even if it runs for a while underground. He'd need force to shift me and no way would he use force on his own mother.

"You'll keep your mouth shut. Understand, dear?" I said that 'dear' as gently and lovingly as I've ever said anything in my life, as I hung on to his hands, until he broke as I knew he would.

"Stop it, Mum, you're frightening me."

"Good lad," I whispered, and let him go.

2

Handle with Care

I'm back in the hospital, tucked up in bed. I don't want to sleep. This has been an extraordinary day. I want to savour and repeat some of it in my head. The sun *was* a dazzling orange orb and it shone on the sea making a pathway, a highway, a wide street paved in gold. Small yachts sailed across this street. They looked like silhouettes cut out of black paper. The sea was so still, dark blue. Only at the very edges where it ran up onto the shingle could you see it still moved...

I saw plenty of sunsets during my last winter at Marine View. Sometimes I walked with Jean in the hour before she had to get back and start preparing dinner. Our walks happened quite naturally, beginning on the Tuesday following Whiz leaving the Home.

I was still able to get about but I relied on my walking stick. I decided to go for a walk. "I'll give it a try," I thought. "The sea is no distance. Down the front path, turn left out of the close and there it is on the other side of the road."

I was in the hall buttoning up my coat when Jean came out of the kitchen.

"Where are you off to, Shirley?"

"The sea front and back."

Jean raised her eyebrows.

"Are you sure?"

I nodded.

"Keep you company?"

I was surprised and pleased but I didn't show it. For the moment I felt Jean wore a sign, 'Handle with Care'.

"I'd appreciate the company."

She put on her camel-coloured duffel coat, threw a scarf round her neck. It was a maroon scarf bought by Whiz, just one of the many presents Whiz bought Jean last Christmas. Jean's mouth tightened.

"Let's go." She opened the front door. "After you, Shirley."

In the time it took me to reach the gate, Jean could have walked to the sea and back, but she kept to my slow pace, hands in her coat pockets, whistling under her breath as if she had all the time in the world. Crossing the road, she took my arm, holding up her hand to stop a white van. The van would have stopped anyway but it was reassuring having Jean in charge. It was a blustery day – light blue sky and shreds of cloud but warm for the time of year, as we say in the Home.

I said little. Jean said even less. I sat in the shelter while Jean settled in front of me on the wooden steps leading down to the beach. We weren't the only ones out; there were plenty of elderly couples. On Worthing sea front you can still see gentlemen in trilby hats, their wives wearing a 'pop-it' tied over tight perms. Not for much longer. Catch sight of them if you can. Old. Elderly. I observed them critically as if I didn't belong to that age group, imagining that their conversation would be on small topics: the purchase of a new bathmat, whether to have boiled or roast potatoes that evening, would the addition of Scholl inner soles make a pair of new shoes more comfortable? Which took me on to thinking of Whiz and Jean and what I'd seen in the kitchen. I couldn't picture any of these old hands cradling Whiz's white breast. I focused on Jean's hands, resting on the knees of her faded denim jeans. They weren't old hands – not yet. An unusual impulse made me reach forward and pat Jean's shoulder. She looked back and smiled at me ruefully as if we'd already had a conversation about what rotten luck it was that my son had held up a mirror in front of them and Whiz hadn't been able to take what she saw reflected.

I risked a question.

"Will Whiz come back?"

"No, Shirley. That's all over."

We didn't walk together every day. Apart from a few odd days like that first Tuesday, it was a wet and stormy winter. Jean often had chores to do and so I'd set off to the beach on my own. Inside I felt as if I was toughening up, but physically I was growing frailer. Everything was becoming a struggle but, by god, I was determined to keep making it. And if I couldn't, you see, the next step was one I didn't want to make. I'd be forced to move from residential home to nursing home, where they line you up in wipe-clean, leatherette armchairs every afternoon and under medication you dream what's left of your life away.

"Shirley, can't you wait till tomorrow? My afternoon's clear and I could walk with you."

Jean stood in my bedroom doorway, watching as I zipped up my boots.

"But Jean, it's a lovely afternoon. The bulbs are coming up."

"While you're admiring the bulbs, you could get mugged."

"Why would anybody want to mug me?"

"Because muggers' preferred victims are old ladies."

"I can't afford to be dependent."

"It's not a matter of dependency. While you're living here, you're my responsibility."

"I can come and go as I please."

A change was taking place between myself and Jean. No longer was I just one of the residents, nor even the favoured resident who'd acted as chaperone while Whiz and Jean had carried on their courtship. Unwittingly Jean was beginning to see me as a friend. As for me, truly, I wasn't only hanging onto my independence to keep my position at Marine View; I was trying to save myself. I'd allowed myself to love Jean. I was frightened, upset, bowled over. I forced myself out onto the sea front on afternoons I'd have far rather been sitting in the kitchen while Jean made her telephone calls or perhaps accompanying her in the car to the supermarket. She needed a friend and I did my best but it would have been so easy to ruin our friendship. If I'd just once blurted out... I so much wanted to call her 'Jean darling'. Linking those two words seemed natural. Once she banged her head on an open cupboard door and I started towards her, my hand outstretched: "Oh Jean da– damn that bloody door. Are you ok?"

I wasn't unhappy. I was happier than I could ever remember being. No bad thing to feel love at eighty years old. It's better to love than be loved. That's what I told myself. My feelings for Jean filled and warmed my breasts like mother's milk. How my son Robert would have recoiled from that idea! "Love, love, love," I hummed to myself, although I'd always detested the Beatles. I wished I knew all the words and made a note to ask Robert about them when he next visited.

*

It wasn't only Jean who missed Whiz. We all did. Within a few days Jean replaced her with a capable, good-natured woman of about fifty, called Maureen. She fitted in nicely but a quirky light had gone out of the Home. No laughter. The rooms felt colder. A home for the elderly is like a painting done in dark, lifeless hues. Whiz had added colour, with her shiny young woman's hair, a lightness of step, a musical voice pitched higher than ours, the stirring up of the air as she rushed about, inspiring in us an interest in her clothes, her Mr Bradley, her bantering with Jean.

Pebbles the cat grew thin. No one noticed at first. In winter the residents turn in on themselves. Even with the central heating radiators pumping out at maximum, we feel the chill in our bones, imagine coughs and colds to be the onset of that feared final illness.

Jean must have noticed something was wrong with Pebbles but she said nothing to us. It was Elsie who put it into words.

"Pebbles has lost weight."

Often we chose to ignore Elsie's pronouncements. Elsie was losing her marbles. However, this statement was in conjunction with Pebbles wandering into the lounge. We were gathered together for afternoon tea. Eagerly we regarded Pebbles, to refute Elsie's opinion. Pebbles was grey and beige. A furry, roly-poly cat ideally suited to a residential home. He was liberal with his favours, appearing to choose each of us in turn to reward with his company. Elsie was right, he had lost weight. His fur was no longer lustrous and his round shape seemed to have fallen inwards to embrace his skeleton. At that moment Jean came in carrying a couple of fresh logs for the fire; she was met with a barrage of concern.

"Ladies, I've tried to tempt him with everything. He's had

breast of chicken, cod, tinned tuna, pilchards, cat treats. He's lost all interest in his food."

"Should he go to the vet?"

"He's booked in for tomorrow."

That evening, Pebbles lay in his basket in the conservatory surrounded by plates of tempting morsels we residents had produced: butter, cream, cheese, Marmite. We came in quietly, whispered, "Good Pebbles. There's a fine boy." If he heard us, he kept his eyes closed. Sometimes his tail twitched.

The next afternoon we watched from the lounge window as Jean's car pulled into the drive. By the time she opened the front door we were all waiting in the hall.

Our small crowd parted to let her through. From the cat basket came a loud irritable wail.

"Well? What did the vet say? Is he going to be all right?"

Without stopping, Jean marched into the kitchen.

"Nothing wrong with him. He's pining."

She shut the kitchen door on us. I gave her five minutes before popping my head round the door.

"Can I come in?"

Jean sat at the table. On the floor by the stove was the cat basket, Pebbles still inside.

"Sit down, Shirley, before you fall down. I'll make tea."

I took my usual chair while Jean switched the gas on under the kettle.

"Shall I let Pebbles out?"

"Whiz is coming for him."

"What?"

"I've rung her. She and the wondrous Paul Bradley are coming over in half an hour."

"But you love Pebbles."

"I am certainly very fond of Pebbles. Unfortunately, along

with apparently everybody else, Pebbles loves Whiz."

"He'll get used to being without her."

"But if he doesn't? If he dies of a broken heart?"

She poured the boiling water into two mugs.

"He's a cat, not a human."

"Cat, human. Shirley, we all have feelings."

She sat down opposite me, running her hand impatiently through her thick hair.

"I'm dreading meeting Paul Bradley. Seeing them both together."

"It might have been worse if you'd bumped into them in the town."

"You're right. Shirley, we haven't talked about what happened. What did you really think? Were you shocked? Disgusted?"

I paused before answering. I had to, because I didn't have any words ready and I wanted to be absolutely honest to myself as well as to Jean.

"Actually I was interested. I've never given... these matters... much thought before. For quite a time I'd been thinking how right the two of you were together, while also thinking, well, that's not the right order of things. I envied what you had. I felt it was foolish, cuddling in here where anybody could walk in, but then perhaps you couldn't help yourselves. I've never been carried away like that. I wish I had."

"Whiz wasn't the same as me. I forced her into it."

"You didn't. You couldn't force her to do what she didn't want to do. She looks young but she's not a child."

The door bell rang and we both started.

Jean swallowed a last gulp of tea, wiped her hands on the seat of her jeans and went out. I heard their voices in the hall. Someone came out of the lounge.

"Whiz, are you coming back?" Doris's voice. I didn't hear Whiz's reply.

Jean led them into the kitchen. I was ready to hate Paul Bradley but he was just a big awkward chap – not unlike a younger version of Robert. Whiz looked different. Her hair was loose on her shoulders, she wore a skirt and blouse I'd never seen before and heeled shoes. When she'd worked with Jean she'd raced everywhere wearing trainers, trousers and sweatshirts. This way she looked more sophisticated. She matched Paul Bradley. Standing together, they looked like a couple beaming out of the local paper announcing their forthcoming engagement or marriage.

"Hello Shirley. Paul, this is Shirley, my favourite resident."

"Hello Shirley. I've heard quite a bit about you."

He shook my hand. He seemed to fill up all the space in the kitchen. Whiz turned almost shyly towards Jean.

"How are you, Jean?"

Jean slid her hands into the pockets of her jeans and rocked on the balls of her feet.

"Fine. Great. Just Mr Pebbles who's not so hot. How about you?"

"I'm fine too." Her voice shook slightly.

Paul Bradley had hunkered down and was peering into the basket.

"Hello, little fellow."

I studied Whiz's face. I wanted to know whether she'd truly loved Jean. For the first time I appreciated how eyes could look 'bottomless', because that's what Whiz's were, as if she'd taken the lid off a well. I knew for certain that the situation was far worse for her than it was for Jean. Whiz had made her choice and it was the wrong one. All her life she'd regret it. Jean had nothing to regret.

Pebbles, hearing Whiz's voice, began to call. Paul Bradley straightened up and grinned at Whiz.

"Don't worry, Pebbles, my Lizzie's come to take you home."

He smiled widely at me. I felt he was almost inclined to pat my neat white curls. He smiled widely at Whiz and then at Jean. Suddenly Whiz looked alarmed. She frowned at him and slightly shook her head. He pinched her cheek like a father might.

"Don't look so agitated, Lizzie. I think we're among friends. Jean, Shirley, I don't know if Lizzie's told you –"

"Paul, I'd rather not –"

"Oh don't be silly. You and Jean have been friends for several years. She should share in our good news, which is: we're expecting a little one in the summer."

"I only found out for sure the other day."

"Lizzie, we had our suspicions at Christmas –"

Paul Bradley found it hard to shut up. He didn't even pause long enough for us to congratulate them. His face was open and innocent and so damned pleased with himself. Abruptly, Jean picked up the cat basket and peered in.

"Goodbye Pebbles. Shirley, say goodbye."

"Goodbye Pebbles."

Paul Bradley strode forward and took the basket.

"He weighs a bit. Hasn't been pining that much."

He grinned at us. Jean ushered them out. I sat back down. My tea was stone cold. Paul Bradley's voice resounded through the hall till finally the front door slammed on his proud, cheerful voice.

As far as I know, Jean never saw Whiz again. I got through the winter. I watched the spring tide washing up over the beach, spattering the shelter with icy spray. As the afternoons lengthened, I had to make for home before the sun had set. Had I known how little time I had, I'd have stayed put, risked catching a cold to watch that gold ball go down in a blaze of glory.

Whenever possible, Jean came with me. If she couldn't make it, I'd see her looking out of the top landing window as I made my way slowly Home-wards. I was too far away to see what I knew to be a look of relief on her face.

One afternoon an ambulance was parked in the drive. I tried to hurry, expecting it to be for Elsie. "Oh poor dear," I thought, "still, she's had a good run for her money." Not Elsie at all. It was Jean. A heart attack. She'd died almost immediately, the doctor told us. At first I couldn't take it in. I thought, loving someone the way I loved Jean, I'd have known by some sixth sense that she wasn't alive any more. I'd feel the gaping hole left in my universe.

Quite a few people came to her funeral. There were family I never knew she had. Of course, all of us residents went. It was doubly sad for us because we were soon to be scattered, as Marine View was being sold to a property developer; luxury flats for the young and healthy. I saw Whiz and Paul Bradley. They didn't come to the service but they stood on the edge of the circle when Jean's coffin was lowered into the ground. She – Whiz – tried to catch my eye, but I couldn't bear to look at her.

I sat in my chair and waited. Where was Robert? He wasn't usually late. Most visiting times he was the first one in the ward. I fixed my gaze on the swing doors while trying to look unconcerned. Finally they opened. In came a very smart middle-aged woman wearing a black coat, a green satin scarf around her neck and knee-high leather boots, the heels hitting the linoleum floor confidently. She stopped in front of me.

"Hello, Mum." The woman laid a bunch of freesias wrapped in lilac tissue paper on my bed before bending down to kiss my cheek.

"Jackie!" I almost blubbed.

"I'm so sorry I haven't been to see you."

"I expect it was difficult."

I reached for the flowers. I buried my face in them. Pink, lilac, white and creamy yellow. I expected no scent but these smelt exactly as freesias should smell.

"I wanted to come." She pulled up Robert's usual chair and sat down facing me.

"I'm so pleased to see you, Jackie." And I was. I'd forgotten how fond I was of my daughter-in-law. Perhaps I'd never known till that moment.

"Well, Robert and I have started... communicating. We may not be capable of living under the same roof, but we've known each other long enough to be friends."

She sat back and looked at me. I cut a rather dismal sight. I regretted not at least having put on a clean cardigan that morning.

"I don't know where Robert's got to. He's usually here by now."

"He is here. He's organising a wheelchair. We thought we'd take you for a drive. Would you like that? Down to the coast. Dear old Worthing. Perhaps look at the Christmas lights in the town centre. There's no Marine View any more, but you might like a breath of sea air."

Jackie's face looked so bright and hopeful. I thought, "Jackie always looked bright and hopeful, and in the old days I couldn't have cared less."

"That's a lovely idea. Particularly the sea front. I'm not bothered about Christmas lights."

The weather was perfect. A sunny winter's day with a breeze blowing – exactly like that first day when Jean came out with me. In the car I daydreamed that I was going back to Jean, as if life was a film I could rewind, playing its few special moments again and again. I saw myself reaching forward to touch Jean's shoulder. That was the only time I'd touched her. She'd bathed me, massaged my pungent lavender oil into my shoulders and joints, tweezered stray hairs from my chin, but Jean had never touched me with any intimacy. Had never wanted to. That was ok. The important thing was that I, Shirley, who had turned her back on physical and emotional contact decades earlier, had done the reaching out. Not much for a lifetime – in fact, sweet f.a. as we used to say in the 1950s – still, a step in the right direction. How many steps do you expect to take after a certain age, anyway?

"Over there, Robert. I always sat in that shelter."

He parked the car and looked back at me.

"Are you up to this, Mother?"

"Yes."

"It's cold."

"Wrap me up well, then."

"She'll be fine. It's what you want to do, isn't it, Mum?"

"It is."

They got me into the wheelchair. Without the nurse to help, it was no easy task for any of us. To avoid the pain, I concentrated on their bent heads as they puffed and panted, as if I weighed several hundredweight, instead of seven and a half stone. Some grey in Robert's hair, Jackie's remained a rich auburn.

"Mum, have you got four legs instead of two?"

They started giggling. They tucked a blanket round my knees, jammed my woolly hat over my ears. The scarf was wound several times round my neck.

"Go easy. I feel like an Egyptian mummy."

"She's got a lot more to say for herself than an Egyptian mummy."

"Who's 'she'? The cat's mother?"

They put on anoraks. They'd truly come prepared. I'd forgotten how efficient Jackie was. She produced a flask of tea and some mince pies while Robert provided the muscle to wheel me up onto the narrow strip of pavement. Somebody was already sitting in the shelter: an old man in an overcoat, a plastic carrier bag of shopping leant against his ankles. Robert hesitated. He's inherited his shyness with strangers from me. Jackie stepped in.

"Come on, he'll probably move once we sit down."

"But is that fair? He got there first."

"Never mind. Really Robert, get pushing!"

The chair began to move again. Just as Jackie predicted, the man did shift.

"Sorry to crowd you out."

"Not at all. I was going anyway."

"See, I said he'd move. He can probably sit in this shelter any day of the week. Cup of tea anyone? Mince pie? They're homemade."

I've told you about the orange sun and the pathway paved with gold, the boats that seemed to be cut from black paper. For a moment, I shut out Robert and Jackie, let their voices slip away. There in front of me was the wooden step where Jean had sat. I saw her still youthful, duffel-coated shoulders, her thick white hair whipped by the wind. Jean. Let it be that day. Let you be sitting on the wooden step and me be reaching out to comfort you. I sniffed.

"Not cold, Mum?"

"Not at all. Do you know, I used to come down here with Jean Matthews?"

"Oh her." Robert frowned and gulped his tea.

"Yes, her."